Distinguishing Facts from Fiction

Facts

Nelle's father did acquire property in Aiken County.

General William Sherman (1820-91) fought in the Civil War as the commanding general of the Union army for 14 years. Sherman's greatest feat was when he marched the Union army across Georgia through South Carolina, destroying much of South Carolina's economic resources. He even marched through Aiken county destroying homes along the way. It is a little known fact that he and his soldiers took silk dresses, tore them to shreds and tied them to their horses! Sherman's army also broke a dam on the Edisto River which was used for transporting logs. The area is now known as Dick Gunter Landing where slave labor was actually used to build a canal connecting to the North Edisto River.

The Edisto Academy opened in 1915 as a two year boarding school which also offered a 12th grade high school education. A railroad town by the name of Seivern once existed there and there is still a Baptist church there which goes by that name.

Nelle was born during the time that her family lived in the academy just before closing because of the effects of the Great Depression.

Dawn is the middle name of Nelle's oldest daughter.

Fiction

Four Oaks, mentioned as a plantation which was destroyed by lightening in a thunder storm, is not a real place.

The Rift of Dawn

By Wynelle Williamson

Blessings!
Wynelle

Copyright © 2005 by Wynelle Williamson

The Rift of Dawn
by Wynelle Williamson

Printed in the United States of America

ISBN 1-59781-635-3

All rights reserved solely by the author. The author guarantees all contents are original and do not infringe upon the legal rights of any other person or work. No part of this book may be reproduced in any form without the permission of the author. The views expressed in this book are not necessarily those of the publisher.

Unless otherwise indicated, Bible quotations are taken from The Living Bible version of the Bible. Copyright 1971 by Tyndale House Publishers, Inc.

All other verses are from the King James version KJV.

www.xulonpress.com

Acknowledgment

I am deeply indebted to my family, including Nancy Shumard, and my dear friend, Barbara Price, for their expertise, loving support, and encouragement in the preparation of this book.

Contents

Chapter 1 — A New Life Begins.............................9
Chapter 2 — Sixteen Years Later..........................15
Chapter 3 — A Few Weeks Later 19
Chapter 4 — Packing for Boarding School 23
Chapter 5 — Edisto Academy 25
Chapter 6 — Return to School............................31
Chapter 7 — Home for Thanksgiving 35
Chapter 8 — The First Snowfall 39
Chapter 9 — Christmas at Edisto.........................43
Chapter 10 — The Telegram 47
Chapter 11 — Graduation Day 53
Chapter 12 — USC 57
Chapter 13 — Wade's Visit 63
Chapter 14 — School Again 67
Chapter 15 — Wedding Day 69
Chapter 16 — A Letter from Dawn 73
Chapter 17 — Alarming News 79
Chapter 18 — Life on the Mission Field Three Years Later 85
Chapter 19 — A Brief Interlude 89
Chapter 20 — Ten Years Later............................93
Chapter 21 — Back Home Again 97
Chapter 22 — The Portrait..............................101
Chapter 23 — The Unveiling.............................107
Chapter 24 — Leaving Again 113

Chapter 25 — The Storm ... 115
Chapter 26 — A Needed Trip Home ... 121
Chapter 27 — An Encounter with Rawl ... 125
Chapter 28 — Transition ... 129
Chapter 29 — A New Year Begins ... 133
Chapter 30 — An Unexpected Afternoon ... 137
Chapter 31 — Deep Thoughts Revealed ... 143
Chapter 32 — Life at Edisto Continues ... 149
Chapter 33 — A Turn of Events ... 151
Chapter 34 — Another Diploma is Earned ... 155
Chapter 35 — The Tapestry ... 159
Chapter 36 — A Letter from Robin ... 165
Chapter 37 — The Big Day Arrives ... 169
Chapter 38 — The Dawning of a New Day ... 171
The Epilogue ... 173

Chapter 1

A New Life Begins

These old gnarled oaks standing almost deserted against the azure sky have known and witnessed a life and world almost forgotten by man. If it were possible, these oaks could relate a beautiful story of the life that they have sheltered below and beyond their spreading branches.

Upon the crest of the hill beyond these oaks, a stately, southern manor once stood. Four tall, white columns upholding the roof of the porch, could clearly be seen from miles around. At one side of this plantation home was a beautiful garden carefully planned and arranged by no one but the plantation mistress. Under her thoughtful supervision each flower and shrub was planted in a perfect location. Crepe Myrtle trees towered over the other tiny plants. At the entrance of the garden were two century plants, carefully watched and eagerly awaited for the time that they would bloom.

It was early in the morning, and each buttercup was filled with the dew that had fallen the night before. The birds had made a choir loft of the tallest tree in the garden and sounded as if they were heralding the entrance of some great event or celebrity. All of a sudden another voice joined the choir of cheerful voices, but this one was different; it seemed to hold the sweetness of a newborn

The Rift of Dawn

baby's cry. Yes, it was, and this sound was coming from the nursery window of the large white house on the hill.

"Yes, Suh, Mister Randall, yo' is the PaPa of a six and a half pound baby girl," came the happy voice of the colored Mammy.

"I knew it, I knew that she'd be a girl. Mrs. Randall never does let me down, and I'll bet she looks exactly like her mother too, doesn't she, Mammy?" replied the proud father.

"Mister Randall, you know yo' can't tell much about newborn babies, but she done got Miz Randall's chestnut brown eyes, and that littl' sprig of hair on top of her sweet littl' head sho does look lack a littl' yellow sunbeam. Come on in here, and I'll show you yo' littl' new Honey Chil'," commanded the waddling woman as she led him down the hall to the nursery smiling from ear to ear.

"Well, it's about time that we had a brown-eyed Randall with Ken and my having blue eyes, Mrs. Randall was being outnumbered," chuckled David Randall as he and Mammy walked down the long hall towards the tiny pink nursery.

David Randall was of English descent. His family had migrated into the Carolinas in the early eighteenth century. He was of average build with broad shoulders that appeared to be capable of shouldering any load. He had a wide forehead and face that narrowed into a determined chin. His hair was medium brown and his eyes were pools of blue that seemed to twinkle when he laughed, which was often.

It was obvious that Mammy adored Mrs. Randall's husband and felt right at home with him now that he was in charge of the Four Oaks Plantation following the death of Virginia's parents who had been her master and mistress previously.

Soon Mammy and David were peering into the crib of the newborn infant. There among the pink and white folds lay the tiny daughter of David and Virginia Randall little realizing that only a little more than a decade ago a civil war was fought on and around the rich fields of her grandfather's Four Oaks Plantation. As a result of David Randall's shrewd judgment and Virginia Randall's wise management, the Four Oaks Plantation had survived the dark storm of war that had so suddenly, and almost completely, demolished a unique and exciting civilization. Only a few years ago this new member of the family would have meant only another mouth to

The Rift of Dawn

feed, but the master and mistress of Four Oaks Plantation had planned and saved to give this little new and only daughter the life of a true southern belle.

"So this is my daughter, the prettiest belle in all Aiken County," smiled Mr. Randall as he proudly looked down into his sleeping daughter's face.

"Yo' know, Mister Randall, that's one thing that's always puzzled me."

"What's that, Mammy?"

"Well, why in the world do they calls this here Achin' County when, except for those mean ol' Yankees coming through, I ain't had an ache or a pain since I wuz raised here on Miz Randall's Pa's plantation. No, siree, I never coulds figger dat out."

"Well, let's just hope that you don't have any more aches and pains as long as this is my plantation, Mammy," laughed Mr. Randall.

"I do believe that she looks exactly like her mother, Mammy. We'll just have to name her Virginia Anne after her mother. And speaking of her mother, when can I see her? Mammy, will you please ask the doctor?" asked David Randall impatiently.

It was at that moment that Dr. Stone opened the door of the bedroom that adjoined the nursery.

Smiling he reached out a hand to David and said, "Congratulations, Mr. Randall, your wife is just fine and so is your baby daughter. She is eager to see you, but she does need her rest."

"Thank you, Doctor, and yes, I am anxious to see her, too," replied David.

"I'll give Mammy some more instructions and will return in a few days to check on Mrs. Randall and the little one. Again, congratulations to you and Mrs. Randall."

After a quick handshake, the doctor started down the stairs as David turned to enter the room to embrace his wife. Virginia appeared weak and tired, but smiled as her husband leaned down to kiss her.

"Have you seen her yet, David?" whispered his wife weakly.

"Yes, I have, and she is just beautiful! Thank you, my Dear. Now our family is complete!" exclaimed David Randall, and he gave his wife a hug.

The Rift of Dawn

It was then that Mammy entered the room with the newest addition to the Randall household. "Littl' Mis' Randall was missing her mama," smiled Mammy with a twinkle in her eye as she laid the tiny bundle in the bassinet beside her mother's bed.

Seeing his little daughter again prompted David Randall to say, "Yes, my Dear, Mammy and I were just discussing her name. I like Virginia Anne, named after you. How about it, Mrs. Randall?"

"I have just been thinking...she must have a name before nightfall," smiled Mrs. Randall.

"But she just can't be named after me since Ken has my maiden name of Kendrick; that would be unfair, David."

"Well, I know just the name, Mister Randall."

"What's that, Mammy? I guess you are entitled to name one of our children," laughed Mr. Randall.

"She'll just have to be called Rose Bud. I declare that little pink turned up nose looks just lack one of Miz Randall's rose buds in the garden," grinned Mammy showing a full set of large white teeth.

"Yes, how is my garden now, Mammy? I haven't been down to see it in weeks. All of my roses must be in full bloom," said Virginia Randall as she looked out the big open window toward the garden below. "Mammy, that's not one of my century plants blooming, is it?" asked Mrs. Randall with a start.

"'fraid it is, Miz Randall, that's me and Mister Randall's secret. We just knowed that it was going to bloom on the day this littl' Honey Chil' wuz born, and it sho did. Littl' Mis' Randall, yo' sho is being honored today!" smiled Mammy as she picked up the new baby in her big black arms.

"Well, that certainly is a surprise! The garden is just perfect now. Look at the dew sparkling in the buttercups, it looks just like millions of tiny diamonds. I do believe that dawn is the loveliest time of the day. I am so glad that our daughter was born at that time of...That's it!!"

"That's what, Virginia, what's wrong?" asked David with a surprised look on his face as he turned toward his wife.

"Dawn, that's what we shall name her. It just suits her perfectly! We'll compromise and name her Dawn Rose Anne. How does that sound to you, Mammy?" smiled Mrs. Randall.

"That sounds fine, and may the Lawd's blessings be on her with whateber name she gets," replied the pleased Mammy.

"And now for approval from the subject in question," commented David Randall as he took his daughter from Mammy's arms. "How does that name sound to you, 'Little Miss Dawn Rose Anne Randall'?"

After a satisfying gurgle, this official name was given to the new comer to the Four Oaks Plantation.

Chapter 2

Sixteen Years Later

Dawn was literally personifying her name as she arose with the sun excited about her upcoming sixteenth birthday celebration. She had looked forward to this day for weeks and now it was almost here.

Dawn had blossomed into a petite and very beautiful young woman. Her golden blonde hair literally bounced around her shoulders as she bounded down the stairs. She ran right into her mother who was quietly ascending the steps to peek in upon her daughter to see if she were awake.

"Oh, Mother, I couldn't sleep; I'm so excited about the plans we are making for my party. Is my dress almost finished? I can hardly wait to try it on."

"Now just slow down, Dear, getting yourself all in a flutter will not make the time pass any quicker," commented Virginia Randall trying to calm her daughter.

In a flash Dawn was in the room admiring her dress that was still on the dress maker's form. It was lovely, made of yellow organdy with brown ribbon insertion flowing around the billowy skirt. More of the insertion was on the bodice lacing a tight fitted waist with a ribbon tied at the top of the skirt.

The Rift of Dawn

"Mother, is it really like the one that you told me was ruined by the Yankees? Oh, tell me that story again, please."

"Well, yes, Dear, it is as well as I can remember. It was nearing the end of the war when a group of Yankee soldiers came meandering up the drive singing and shouting as they approached the house. Instead of destroying anything, they were more in a festive mood taking some of my silk dresses and this yellow one in particular, tearing them into shreds and tying them on their horses manes and tails as streamers. They left almost as quickly as they came.

Shortly after that, we heard that General Lee had surrendered at Appomattox Court House in Virginia. We were fortunate that this house survived the war; however, we did lose the mill pond when Sherman's men came through earlier and destroyed the dam. We could then so longer grind our wheat into flour or grind the corn into meal or grits."

"Oh, yes, Mother, the fact that the house was spared when so many others were burned when Sherman's men came through on their march to Columbia was a miracle!" exclaimed Dawn. "And that's how you and PaPa came to live here because Grandpa Randall's home was burned, wasn't it?"

"Yes, that's true! Even though there was not much left but the house, we were grateful to have a roof over our heads," said Mrs. Randall with a pensive look in her eye. "Also to have Mammy and Dawson stay on with us. They were just too scared to leave and preferred life here with us instead of the unknown. That's how they became almost family to us. How thankful we were that they did since your grandfather, my father, was killed in the war, and Mother really grieved herself to death a few years later! Losing my father and the life that she had always known was just too much for her to bear. We barely got by until your Father and I were married, and he came here to live and manage the farm.

The Yankee soldiers had beaten and bent the family's saws, that had been used to cut timber, to the point that they were no longer useable. It took your father many tries before he was able to get one in shape to saw again. With Reconstruction and so much building going on, David was able to revive the lumber business. Using the man-made canal that was built with the former slave labor, he was

The Rift of Dawn

able to float logs down the North Edisto River to the lumber yards in Charleston."

"That's enough about sad things! Just how many of your friends did you invite to this party?" inquired her Mother.

Dawn rolled her eyes in a sheepish sort of way and replied, "Oh, not more than a dozen of my closest friends. Do you remember, my friend at school, Alice Stewart? She asked if she could bring her cousin, Wade, since he will be visiting her family and possibly transferring to our school in the fall."

"Sure, Dear, the more the merrier. It's your birthday after all," called Mrs. Randall as she started down the hall to begin the day's activities.

Chapter 3

A Few Weeks Later

"Miz Dawn, if you don't stand still, I'll never get these ribbons tightened on this weskit. Jes give me a few more minutes," pleaded Mammy.

"I know! I know! Mammy, it's just that I want to be down stairs when the first guest arrives," replied Dawn with one hand on the doorknob as she impatiently patted her tiny slender foot on the bedroom floor.

"You will be, I promise!" Pulling the ribbons more tightly and checking to measure that the ends were even, Mammy, feeling satisfied, at last tied a bow at the waist. "There now, I'm all finished. Take a look in this mirror and see how pretty yo' looks," admired the panting woman to the impatient girl standing before her.

Intending to pause for a passing glance in the full length mirror, the young girl stopped to take in the reflection before her revealing a very beautiful young lady. Her hair had been pulled back from her face and held up on either side with combs attached to brown ribbons that matched the ribbons on her dress. Her blonde tresses were fashioned in curls in the back. The yellow organdy dress was slightly off the shoulders, while the creamy folds of the skirt fell softly to the floor.

Feeling pleased with what she saw in the mirror, Dawn asked, "Mammy, is that really me? It is prettier than I even imagined!"

The Rift of Dawn

"It sho is you, Chil'! Yo' is going to be the Belle of the Ball tonight. That yo' is!" exclaimed Mammy.

Dawn was brought to reality as she heard her mother call from downstairs that the first guests had arrived. Mrs. Randall, a very petite, but gracious hostess was eager to greet the friends of her daughter as they arrived for the party. Her light blonde hair framed her oval face and chestnut brown eyes. Her slender hands and feet were in constant motion as she fulfilled the duties of the mistress of the Four Oaks Plantation.

Soon there was a room filled with gayly, chattering young voices. Dawn in her usual vivacious way was welcoming each guest and making sure that everyone was having a good time.

Before long she realized that her good friend, Alice, was not among the group nor her cousin, Wade. She did so want to meet him after Alice had given her such a glowing description of him. She was stopped abruptly in her daydreaming when she noticed her mother coming toward her with Alice and a tall, dark, nice looking young man. He was of a tall, slender build and appeared to be quick on his feet.

"Dawn," she heard her mother call, "this is Wade, Alice's cousin, from the upper part of the state."

As she approached this new acquaintance, Dawn noticed that his eyes were greenish blue but somewhat sad.

"Hello, Wade, welcome to Four Oaks. I'm glad that you could come," announced the vivacious sixteen-year-old with a sparkle in her eye.

Immediately, she saw a change in Wade's expression when she came into his presence.

It was obvious that Wade was smitten with Dawn and did his best to monopolize her attention. She did her best to make him feel welcomed, but as the hostess, she had been taught to circulate among the other guests, also, which she did as much as Wade allowed. Soon it was time to cut the birthday cake and serve the refreshments in the dining room.

The evening passed quickly as the young people enjoyed the fellowship of one another. Some danced while the others sat quietly talking. They spoke excitedly about the approaching fall school term at Edisto Academy which was only a few weeks away.

Mrs. Randall mingled among the young guests making each one feel welcomed. As she approached Wade, she commented, "I understand that you may be attending the academy in the fall."

"Yes, Ma'am," he replied, "I have already been accepted. They do have the courses that I plan to take there."

"And what would that be?" queried Mrs. Randall with an interested smile.

"Oh, I plan to take some theology courses and a foreign language, probably Spanish," answered Wade excitedly as he realized that Dawn's mother was really interested in his plan of study.

"It sounds as if you may be thinking about foreign missions."

"Yes, I am, Mrs. Randall, I believe that God is leading me in that direction."

"That is wonderful! The academy has some fine teachers in that field. I'm sure that they will guide you in the right direction."

"Yes, I agree. It should be an exciting year," replied Wade as he turned to smile at Dawn who was coming over to where the two of them were talking.

"Have you enjoyed the evening, Wade? I hope that you have become acquainted with all my friends since most of them will be at the academy."

With this statement from Dawn, Mrs. Randall excused herself to respond to the guests who were starting to the door to leave.

"It's been a wonderful party, Mrs. Randall, but we must be leaving. Thanks so much for having us," said one of the guests.

Soon all the guests had left except Alice and her cousin, Wade, who was still lingering around Dawn.

"Isn't it exciting, Dawn? You're now 'Sweet Sixteen'! What fun we're going to have this next school year! Wade appears to be quite fascinated with you," whispered Alice as she hugged her best friend goodbye.

As the door closed behind the last guests, Dawn slumped into a large winged-back chair to reflect upon the evening.

"It was a super party, Mother, thanks. I believe that everyone had a great time. I can hardly wait until we're all together at the academy in the fall," said Dawn as she smiled at her mother before climbing up the stairs.

"Being sixteen is a wonderful time of life!" thought Mrs. Randall.

Chapter 4

Packing for Boarding School

"Dawson, will you come and help me get my trunk closed?" called Dawn as she sat on top of the bulging trunk in the middle of the bedroom floor. All around her were still unpacked items that were left discarded for lack of room in the trunk. "Somehow I will just have to get by without them," thought Dawn.

"Sho 'nough, Missy," answered the smiling Darky as he entered through the tall oak bedroom door. Seeing the young girl about to slide off the trunk lid, he could not help but reply, "Miz Dawn, what do you have in here? Yo' is planning to come home fer the holiday season, aren't you? It appears that yo' is going away fer good!"

Seeing the twinkle in his eye, she caught the lightheartedness of the moment. "Oh, Dawson, you know that I could never miss coming home for the holidays. With Mammy's delicious cooking and Mother's wonderful holiday decorations, nothing could keep me away...absolutely nothing!"

At that moment Mrs. Randall appeared in the doorway with an anxious look on her face, "Dawn, aren't you through packing yet? Your father will be here soon ready to hitch up Dobbin to take you to the academy."

The Rift of Dawn

As Virginia Randall stood surveying the room, Dawn noticed that her mother wiped a tear from her eye. Running to her side with a quick hug, she cried, "Oh, Mother, don't be sad, I'll be back in a few months for Thanksgiving and then Christmas. There will be so much that I will have to tell you then."

"Of course, you are right, Dear, it's just that we're going to miss you so much. This room and the house just won't be the same without you."

As the two women, mother and daughter, started down the hall, Mrs. Randall called out over her shoulder, "Just leave the trunk, Dawson, until Mr. Randall comes to help you load it onto the buggy."

At that moment Mammy came through the doorway with a basket filled with goodies, some of Dawn's favorites. "Here, Chil', take these with you. Yo' is bound to get hongry on the way," encouraged Mammy as she handed the basket to Dawn.

"I'm sure that she will, Mammy, I don't believe that she has eaten a thing this morning," pondered Mrs. Randall.

"You're right, Mother, I have been much too excited to eat. I sure am going to miss these every morning, Mammy," sighed Dawn as she eyed a ham biscuit under the linen napkin. "I wonder what we will have for breakfast at the academy this year?"

"Miz Dawn, Your PaPa is here, and the trunk is already in the buggy. You had best say your "goodbyes" and get in the buggy, too," ordered Dawson.

Giving her mother and Mammy a goodbye hug, the young woman whispered, "I love you," to each of them and skipped down the steps and along the path to where the horse and buggy were waiting.

She turned to wave goodbye. It was at that moment that she saw Mammy pick up the corner of her big white apron and wipe a tear from her eye.

Chapter 5

Edisto Academy

The day was bright and sunny as Dobbin, the spirited Randall horse, clip clopped down the dusty road toward the academy. It was too early in the season to notice any change in the fall foliage; however, there was an unusual crispness in the air on this September morning.

Dawn was too excited about the upcoming school year and seeing old friends as well as anticipating meeting some new ones to notice as they passed by the depot of the small, but thriving town on the Southern Railroad. There departing from the train was a group of students who, too, were coming to experience a school year of life at the academy.

Soon the horse and buggy approached the academy. Two large brick columned structures flanked the entrance to the drive toward the campus. A curved wrought iron archway supported large wooden letters, EDISTO ACADEMY, above the entrance to the main driveway.

Dawn's heart began to beat faster as they drove under the archway down the live oak drive toward the main building which also housed the girls' dormitory.

It was obvious that she was not the first to arrive. Students were already unloading trunks and boxes at both the boys' and girls' dormitories. Dawn quickly surveyed the group hoping to see a familiar face.

The Rift of Dawn

As Mr. Randall guided the horse, he looked for an empty hitching post. Dawn eagerly scanned the students who were scattered about the campus and looked for her good friend, Alice.

Meanwhile, Alice spotted her and called out, "I'm over here, Dawn, by the summer house."

"Hi, Alice! I can't believe that we are back at last!" cried Dawn eager to depart from the buggy and hug her friend.

Soon they were arm in arm and headed toward the registration office to check in.

"You look great, Dawn! I couldn't wait to tell you how much Wade and I enjoyed your party. Wade was quite smitten with you and has not stopped talking about you. He is excited about seeing you again when he arrives. He should have arrived on the morning train," exclaimed Alice as they quickly walked down the hall looking for their dormitory room after having received their new room assignments.

"There it is, Room 218, at the end of the hall. Oh, I am so glad that it overlooks the gazebo on the front lawn. That is a happening place and so much fun to watch who meets who there," observed Dawn as she propped her arms on the window sill trying to see who was already there.

The afternoon hours seemed endless as the girls unpacked all of their boxes and trunks. They were tired after getting everything in place and were glad to hear the evening supper bell ring. There was quite a flurry of activity as the girls on the second floor hurried to the dining hall.

It was customary that at the first meal of each new semester the students were allowed to choose their own places at the table, so naturally they wanted to be near the front of the line before all of the best seats were taken.

"Look, Dawn, there is Wade now. He did arrive on the morning train. Come over here, Wade, we have a place for you at our table," called Alice.

Hearing the sound of her voice brought a ready smile to his face as he turned to see her. It was obvious that he was also looking to see if Dawn were there with her. And she was! When she saw him, she pointed to an empty seat beside her.

The Rift of Dawn

Steaming bowls of vegetable soup and big chunks of cornbread soon brought a brief lull in the chatter that had previously filled the dining room. The excitement of seeing old friends and the prospect of meeting new ones made the first evening meal at the academy pass very quickly. Before leaving the dining hall, the students were reminded that they had only one hour before they should meet in the auditorium for their first orientation meeting.

As they left the dining hall some of the students and faculty lingered in the halls renewing old acquaintances. Dawn and Alice went out into the adjoining courtyard and were soon followed by Wade.

"Wait up, Dawn and Alice!" called out Wade as he quickly caught up with them. Being a member of the track team at his former school made him move in a flash. "I really enjoyed the party at your place recently, Dawn, and have been looking forward to being with you here at the academy. We'll have to check our schedules to see if we have any classes together."

"Oh, yes, let's do. Alice and I have already checked ours, and we do have some together, especially the early morning ones. But I do need someone to help me stay awake during the warm afternoons. You see, I'm a morning person," smiled Dawn, glancing toward Alice with a knowing look on her face.

"She sure is," replied Alice, "if it weren't for me last year, she would never have made it through that last class in the afternoon."

"Now, Alice," laughed Dawn with a twinkle in her eye, "I wasn't that bad, was I?"

"Oh, well, maybe I was stretching a point, but just barely," admitted her best friend.

"Let's change the subject. Wade, have you done anything exciting since we last saw you?" asked Dawn.

After thinking for a moment, Wade replied, "Not really, just the usual things that you have to do to close out the summer and get ready for a term away at school. Oh, yes, I did have one last track meet at my former school."

"Really?" Alice asked excitedly, "How did you do?"

"Came in first place actually!"

"That's great, Wade, you must be a pretty fast runner!" exclaimed Dawn as she glanced at her watch. "Oh, my, we only

The Rift of Dawn

have about fifteen minutes before time for our meeting in the auditorium."

Quickly Alice started toward their dorm room, "Wade, we'll see you shortly. Dawn and I need to freshen up a bit before the meeting."

As they began to part company, Wade winked at Dawn. "Save me a seat in case I'm late," he called over his shoulder.

"Oh, you won't be," laughed Dawn. "You're a track star, remember?"

The auditorium was almost filled when Dawn and Alice entered for the orientation meeting. They were about to slip into two empty seats near the back when Alice saw Wade motioning for them to come near the front where he had been saving them two seats. Just as they slid in beside him, the faculty began to appear on the stage.

"That was close!" whispered Alice. "It takes a few minutes longer to come from our room at the end of the hall."

Mr. Washburn, the president, rose and gave his usual signal for the student body to come to order. "Faculty and students, we want to welcome you to another school year here at Edisto Academy. As is customary, we'll begin by singing our school's alma mater; however, we will have someone new directing it. Let me introduce to you Mr. Covell's assistant, Rawl Manning, who will be completing some college credit work with us this first semester. He will also be assisting in the Fine Arts department with some of our art classes. Mr. Manning, come now and lead us."

Having come into the auditorium at the last minute, Dawn had not noticed until now that there was someone new on the platform. She could not help but be attracted to his striking features: blonde hair, a prominent square chin, stately nose, and piercing blue eyes. It was obvious from his tanned skin that he had spent a good bit of time outdoors making a noticeable difference between his blonde hair and tanned olive complexion to say nothing of his captivating smile showing beautiful even white teeth.

The Rift of Dawn

The student body was half way through the singing of the alma mater before Dawn realized that she had not sung the first note. She had been so entranced by this charming newcomer to the academy staff.

The remainder of the meeting was spent in introducing the faculty and reviewing the rules and policies of the school. Since Dawn would be graduating at the end of this term, she was familiar with them and instead centered her attention on Rawl as he sat with the other faculty members. He did appear to be confident in his new role. She wished that she had signed up for an art class, but then there was always the chorus. Surely he would be helping Mr. Covell with that.

"Yes," thought Dawn, "this is going to be an interesting year, indeed it will!"

Chapter 6

Return to School

The first week of school had been extremely busy, as the students familiarized themselves with the new classes and faculty. Already it seemed that each teacher must have thought that his class was the only one that the students had because Dawn and the others already felt overwhelmed with assignments.

As the close of the afternoon study hour drew near, Dawn realized that she must have a breath of fresh air before time for the evening meal. She slipped down the back stairs to walk out to her favorite spot on campus and maybe, just maybe, no one else would be there at this time of day. She could tell that the days were getting shorter, and it would soon be sundown. As luck would have it, there seemed to be no one else outside, so she hurried to the gazebo just as the sun began to sink behind the clouds in the west.

To her surprise, she was not alone in her favorite place on campus. There was Rawl Manning beside an easel with a partial painting of the evening sunset. He appeared to be just as startled to see her.

"Well, hello," he smiled, "I see that someone else enjoys watching the sun go down, also. I didn't realize that the study hour was over already."

The Rift of Dawn

Dawn heard a bit of sarcasm in his voice as a slight reprimand that she was not using the entire hour for study so early in the school year.

"Oh, it isn't quite yet! I just needed a breath of fresh air and getting to see the sunset was as good excuse as any to stop a bit early. It is beautiful, isn't it? And you're doing such a wonderful job of capturing it on canvas," replied Dawn a little embarrassed that someone had found her not studying the entire hour. "I think that it would be difficult to seize the fading colors of the sun's rays, but you seem to be bringing them to life in your painting in such a realistic way. Do you always paint landscapes, or do you ever do other subjects?"

"As a matter of fact, I do," replied Rawl revealing a spark of interest on his face as he realized that she was genuinely interested in his work. "My ultimate goal is to do portraits. It is my desire to portray through a person's eyes their true feelings and personality.

"You have very expressive eyes and quite an unusual color combination of blonde hair and deep brown eyes, I might add."

"Why, thank you! My father has said the same thing about me. He often remarked that he was glad that I was a brown-eyed Randall since he and my older brother have blue eyes!" exclaimed the surprised young woman.

In the distance the sound of the supper bell could be heard ringing just as the last of the paling rosy glow of the sun's rays began to sink behind the tree tops on the western side of the campus.

"Oh, is it supper time already?" remarked Dawn. "I have so enjoyed sharing the sunset with you and seeing how well you have preserved it on canvas. I almost wish that I had signed up for one of Mr. Covell's classes and learned more from you."

"It has been a pleasure sharing these moments with you, also and possibly getting to know a potential future portrait subject," he said with a twinkle in his eye. "I still have another class to take at the university in that area before I get serious about that kind of work.

"Have a good evening," said Rawl as he turned to gather up his paints and brushes. After pausing a moment, he turned back to Dawn and inquired, "By the way, you have an advantage over me. I don't know your name, only that you are a Randall."

"Oh, please forgive me, I'm Dawn, Dawn Randall," she replied over her shoulder as she started toward the dining hall.

Rawl took one last glance at her and noticed that a fading golden ray of sunlight brought out the highlights in her hair as twilight began to slowly fill the summer house.

Dawn sat quietly preoccupied with the recent events of the afternoon on her mind during supper while the others chattered away about the day's activities. It was somewhat noticeable to Wade so he remarked, "Cat got your tongue?"

Not wanting to admit that she had slipped out of her room during the last part of study hour, she hastily replied, "Oh, I'm sorry, just thinking about all that has been happening lately. Do you feel overwhelmed with school work already?" hoping this change of subject would get the spotlight off her for a while.

"Boy, do I, I'll sure be burning the midnight oil this year. At this rate there won't be much time for fun and games," announced Wade as he turned to leave.

After Wade left, the two girls started back toward their dorm room. Linking her arm around Dawn, Alice commented, "Dawn, I agree with Wade, you did seem a bit preoccupied this evening and not your usual bubbly self. Anything wrong or did something happen when you went out during study hour?"

"Well, yes, it did! I didn't want to say anything while Wade was with us," answered Dawn.

With her curiosity aroused following that statement, Alice quickly commented, "Do tell, what happened?"

Dawn didn't need much prompting because she was almost bursting to tell her best friend. "Alice, you know how I love the gazebo, so I had gone there to observe the sunset, and guess who was there with his paints and easel painting the gorgeous sunset?"

"Who? Who? Tell me!"

"None other than Mr. Rawl Manning. He is really quite fascinating! We had a wonderful chat. He said that I had very expressive eyes. He even implied that he might sometime like to do a portrait of me."

"Really? He actually said that?" replied Alice taking it all in.

"He really did and hopefully he won't report me for skipping out on the last few moments of study time. I sure don't need any demerits this early in the school year," announced Dawn with a look of apprehension on her face.

"Well, I can see that he made quite an impression on you. It probably was a smart idea not to mention it to Wade. He can be quite jealous if he feels threatened," responded Alice.

"Now, Alice, Wade has nothing to worry about. Mr. Manning is a part of the faculty, you know, and will be here just until the end of the first semester, but I can dream, can't I?" smiled Dawn as she squeezed Alice's hand before closing their dorm room door as the two girls retired for the evening.

Chapter 7

Home for Thanksgiving

"It's hard to believe that it is already the day before Thanksgiving," thought Dawn as she waited impatiently for her brother, Ken, who was coming to take her home for the fall break. Some of the others who lived farther away had already left earlier that morning.

There had been a flurry of activities during the beginning of the fall semester. So much had happened in such a short time. She and Wade had become close friends and quite often attended the chapel services each morning together as well as the Sunday worship service at the community church across the road from the academy. Immediately after supper, a vesper prayer service was held in each dormitory, conducted by the faculty and students; however, they were unable to share this time together since they resided in separate dorms.

Reflecting upon these events, Dawn let her day dreams remind her of the time that Rawl came with Mr. Covell to conduct the evening vespers at the girls' dormitory. Rawl recognized her in the group and invited her and the others, of course, to audition for the Edisto Choral Club. Taking him up on the offer, she found to her surprise that she was accepted. It had been fun at the practice sessions, and she had learned a lot about music. She was looking forward to their Christmas concert.

The sound of horses' hooves brought her back to reality. Looking up she saw Ken and Dobbin. Jumping from her suitcase where she had been perched for the wait, Dawn flew quickly down the steps and into her brother's arms.

"Hello, Ken, it is so good to see you. I feel like it has been ages since we have been together," squealed Dawn.

"My, you have grown into quite a lovely young woman! I'm sorry that Pa Pa and I missed your 'Sweet Sixteen' party, but lumberyard business in Charleston kept us from being with you. You were in our thoughts," said Ken with all smiles for his 'favorite' sister.

"I know, I wish that you could have been there, too, and met some of my friends," replied Dawn.

"And where are your friends? I heard that they are here with you at school. I especially wanted to meet Wade to see if I approve," smiled her brother with a wink.

"You're too late, they left early this morning because they had farther to travel. Maybe you'll see them when you bring me back."

Reaching for Dawn's valise, Ken remarked, "This is yours, isn't it? Let's get going. Everyone is eager to see you and hear about what you have been doing."

The time passed quickly during the drive from the academy to Four Oaks as the two young people caught up on the happenings in each of their lives. Before long, Ken was hitching up Dobbin beside one of the large live oak trees in front of the Randall's large white house that was located at the top of the hill.

At that moment, one of the big oak front doors opened, and Dawson came toward them to help with Dawn's belongings. "Welcome home, Missy!" smiled Dawson as Dawn flew into his arms with a great big hug.

"It's so good to be home, Dawson. How is everyone?" responded a very happy young lady.

"We'se all fine, that's fer sure, now that you'se home!" he exclaimed as he picked up Dawn's luggage from the back of the buggy. "Your Ma and Mammy are inside making sure that everything is just right fer you. You sure have been missed. Yes, Ma'am!"

Bounding up the steps two at a time, Dawn was soon in the arms of her mother with a smiling Mammy right behind her waiting her turn to give her a big hug.

It was so good to be home even if it were for just a few days.

Dawn was awakened the next morning with the smells of the Thanksgiving dinner filling the house. The aroma of spices mixed with the smell of the turkey baking in the warm oven made her realize that she really was home. It didn't take her long to get dressed and hurry down the stairs.

"My, what smells so good?" was her greeting as she entered the warm kitchen.

"Good morning, Sleepyhead! We thought you were going to sleep away the day," teased Ken as he added more wood to the stove.

"Oh, don't tease your sister, Ken. We wanted you to get your beauty rest," smiled her mother as she gave her daughter a hug. "What would you like for breakfast?"

"Know what I would really like?"

"No, what?"

"Some of Mammy's ham biscuits. Nothing at school tastes as good as those," answered Dawn as she sat down at the table.

Smiling as she brought a big platter piled high with ham biscuits, the black woman replied, "I guessed that you might say that and had some ready for yo'." Always eager to please her favorite girl she set the platter in front of Dawn and said, "Here yo' are, Honey Chil'. Yo' do looks kinda thin. Ain't they been feedin' you there at dat school?"

"Of course, Mammy, but not as good as you do! They have kept us very busy this fall. It's a wonder that we have time to eat at all," answered Dawn as she bowed her head to offer 'Thanks' before eating.

The Rift of Dawn

The rest of the morning was filled with questions about school which Dawn was eager to talk about- classes, new friends, old friends, activities, and of course, the excitement of the upcoming Edisto Choral Christmas Concert.

"You have had an exciting beginning to this school year. Now you just be sure to spend your time studying and not all socializing. Remember you will be entering college next fall," encouraged her mother.

"Ken, please see if your father has finished with the animals and tell him that dinner is ready to be served in the dining room."

The table in the dining room was laden with a bountiful supply of food—the succulent turkey waiting to be carved, sweet potatoes that had been preserved in the potato bank, green beans and corn that had been canned from the summer garden, as well as various kinds of squash.

Along the sideboard were freshly baked pumpkin pies among other desserts just waiting to be enjoyed by the family.

David Randall had taken time to freshen up before joining his family in the dining room. After each family member was seated at the table, Mr. Randall bowed his head to give 'Thanks' for the bountiful blessings that they had enjoyed during the year. They were also thankful that the entire family was together again at the plantation during this holiday season.

Thanksgiving weekend passed much too quickly for Dawn and soon she was saying, "Goodbye," again, but not for long because Christmas was just a few weeks away. That was always a joyous occasion at the Four Oaks Plantation and one that she would eagerly anticipate.

Chapter 8

The First Snowfall

After arriving back at school, Dawn and the others soon fell into the routine of studying and schedules. Much of her time was devoted to extra practices for the Edisto Choral Club concert. It had been planned to coincide with the final day of the fall term so parents and friends could come for the concert and then take their students home for the holidays.

Dawn had mixed emotions about the concert. She was excited because they had worked very hard in their practice sessions and were looking forward to performing their best that afternoon; however, because this would also close out the fall term, it would also be Rawl's last day at the academy while on staff. A reception following the performance was being planned in his honor as well as for the parents and guests who would attend the concert. It was going to be a day that she didn't want to miss.

Soon the sounds as well as the smells of Christmas began to appear around the campus. Fresh pine garlands had been draped around the outside of the summer house. Cedar and holly with bright red berry wreaths adorned the entrance to the academy and also the doors of the main buildings. It was not unusual to pass a student in the hallway and hear the humming of a Christmas carol, most likely one that would be sung in the upcoming concert. It was really getting harder and harder to concentrate on studies.

The Rift of Dawn

Just as Dawn had finished her last class and started back to her dorm room, she heard someone calling her name. It was then that she saw Wade coming toward her. "Wait up, Dawn!" he called, "I was hoping to see you before your practice this evening. Could you meet me at the summer house for a few minutes, I have something for you?"

"Why sure, Wade, just let me take these things by my room, and I'll meet you there in about ten minutes."

"Better get your heavy coat and scarf. It's getting really cold out," called back Wade as he headed toward his dorm.

There was a bone chilling crispness in the air on this mid-December afternoon. It was rare to have snow this far south before Christmas; however, the overcast sky did look threatening.

Wade was back in a flash with a small package inside his coat pocket. Looking around, he was relieved to see that there was no one in the gazebo at the moment, but then it was extremely cold out. He did wish that Dawn would hurry. He could hardly wait to see how she liked his surprise.

Wade noticed that the wind was getting up as it blew some of the last of the fall leaves across the gazebo floor. He felt a chill against his neck. "I should have taken my own advice and gotten my scarf, too," he thought.

It was then that he heard Dawn's footsteps coming up behind him. "I'm sorry, Wade, have you been waiting very long in this cold? Mr. Covell asked me to take some music by the practice room for him. We are to practice thirty minutes earlier this evening since this will be our final rehearsal."

"Oh, no, just a few minutes. It just seems long any time I'm waiting for you," he said with a wink.

"Why did you want to see me, Wade? I'm curious," questioned Dawn with a shiver while clutching her scarf closer around her neck.

"This is why," answered Wade as he pulled a small gayly wrapped package from his pocket and handed it to her.

"Oh, Wade, I didn't expect this," said Dawn excitedly. "I haven't been anywhere to get you anything."

Quickly, the paper and ribbon were removed and the small box opened. Inside was a lovely gold necklace with a dainty little cross pendant.

"I wanted you to have it to wear in the concert tomorrow. Here let me put it on you," insisted Wade.

After fastening the clasp, Wade gave Dawn a quick hug and wished her a Merry Christmas.

"Thanks, Wade, I really do like it, and it will be perfect for the Christmas concert tomorrow. You are staying for it, aren't you?"

"Oh, I wouldn't miss it! That's for sure," he added.

Reaching toward the sky, Dawn squealed excitedly, "Was that a snowflake I just felt on my face? Wouldn't it be just perfect to have a White Christmas!" exclaimed Dawn.

"We had better get you inside before you catch your death of cold and then not be able to sing tomorrow," replied Wade as they hurried toward the main building.

Snow fell softly for the remainder of the afternoon and was still falling at twilight when it was getting too dark to see the fluffy white crystal shapes as they floated silently to the ground. Luckily, a full moon reflected the white winter wonderland later that evening.

Coming from the final rehearsal, Dawn was a little concerned that the inclement weather would keep some from attending the final semester performance of the Edisto Choral Club the following day.

Chapter 9

Christmas at Edisto

The auditorium was filled with proud parents and interested guests eagerly awaiting the opening curtain of the Christmas concert. Lighted candles and pine boughs decorated each window sill as well as the stage. Everything really did reflect the Christmas spirit throughout the room.

On stage behind the curtain, Dawn stood in her place ready for the opening number. Rawl looked dashing as ever as he stood poised and ready to direct the first half of the concert. He smiled as he stepped forward to greet the audience and announce the first selection.

As soon as the curtain opened Wade scanned the choral group looking for Dawn. There she was standing radiantly in the second row. "Was she wearing the cross pendant that he had given her?" Looking closely, he saw it sparkle in the reflection of the candlelight which matched his big Stewart smile.

She really was becoming very special to him, but he thought, "Does she feel the same way about me?" Only time would tell, and he would have to be patient.

Following the brief intermission, Wade let his imagination wander during the final part of the program. With college, seminary, and final preparation for the mission field lying ahead, could he dare to believe that Dawn was to be a part of this dream with him? He would have to pray about this and trust God for the outcome.

The curtain's closing after the final bow brought Wade back to the moment as he stood with the others to go to the reception in the dining hall.

Meanwhile Dawn and the choral members were behind stage saying their farewells to Rawl and presenting him with a plaque to remind him of his days there at the academy.

Dawn's heart beat faster as it became her turn to speak personally to him. She did so want him to know how much she had appreciated all that he had taught her about music and that she would look forward to a future time when he could possibly paint a personal portrait of her.

She was pleased that she had been able to express her thoughts without sounding too much like a silly school girl.

"Yes, Miss Randall, it has been a real pleasure having you in the choral group, also. Mr. Covell and I have commented on your accomplishments here in the music department. And maybe our paths will cross again when I can claim to be an accomplished portrait artist," smiled Rawl with his familiar dashing smile as he turned to greet the next student.

Quickly Dawn hurried to the dining hall to join Wade and Alice. Her parents and Ken were there, also. Wade had said that he wanted to meet her brother. Thanks to Alice, they were all together and seemed to be enjoying each other's company.

"Hello, everybody!" called Dawn as she joined the group, "How did you like the concert?"

"It was just great, Honey. All of your voices blended together so well," answered her mother as she gave her daughter a big hug.

"I'm so glad that you all are here. I wasn't sure if the weather would keep people away, but the auditorium appeared to be full. Wade, I see that you have met my father and Ken."

The Rift of Dawn

"Oh, yes, Alice took care of us while you were busy," smiled Wade as he reached for her hand and gave it a squeeze to let her know how special she was to him.

It was then that Alice spoke up to remind him that they needed to be going. It was almost time to catch the train home for the holidays. "It was so nice seeing all of you again, but we must be going, Wade. Merry Christmas to all of you." After giving Dawn a quick good-bye hug, she and Wade excused themselves through the crowd.

Mr. Randall reminded his family that they too must be going. The snow had stopped, but nightfall was just a few hours away.

Dawn had never felt so cold in her life as they rode up the tree-lined drive to the Randalls' home on the hill. In the moonlight she could see that all the trees were blanketed with snow. It was truly a winter wonderland; nevertheless, she felt chilled to the bone.

Thanks to Dawson and Mammy there was a nice fire roaring in the fireplace and mugs of hot chocolate awaiting them as they entered the house removing their outer wraps and scarves.

Later as the family returned to their normal activities, Dawn sat beside the fire covered in a warm shawl and reflected upon the events of the last few weeks. Her eyes were drawn to the flames of the fire as they lovingly curled around the huge log in the back of the fireplace.

Occasionally a spark would fly upward as if to say to the burning flame, "I want to be released and soar higher." She wondered, "Was this a parallel to her life? Oh, how she wanted to follow God's plan and not just Wade's plan for her life."

The coziness of the warm fire and the sipping of the hot cocoa caused Dawn's eye lids to become heavy and before she knew it she was being awakened by her mother to be told that it was time for bed. As she trudged up the stairs to bed, she decided not to make any decisions tonight because after all she had come home to enjoy the holidays, and that was what she intended to do.

The next few days were filled with the usual before-Christmas preparations, baking, Christmas package surprises, and decorating. Each year, Mrs. Randall brought in evergreens from the surrounding woods, and this year she dusted them with flour to resemble the recent snow that had blanketed the area so beautifully. She made garlands for the mantel and wreaths for the front doors.

It was customary to invite some of the nearby neighbors in for an evening of celebration.

Carols were sung and everyone enjoyed Mammy's baking, especially her plum pudding. Mrs. Randall served wassail from the sideboard in the dining room.

Usually Dawn enjoyed the occasion, but since none of her academy friends would be in the group, she wasn't as excited as she once was. But then some of Ken's friends would be there, and she always enjoyed their company.

The rest of the holidays came and went. Dawn found herself looking forward to her return to the academy. She wasn't sure why, since Rawl would no longer be there, and she only had one more semester before graduation. Maybe she was looking forward to seeing Wade again.

Chapter 10

The Telegram

Returning to the academy, Dawn found that she was soon absorbed in the activities of the spring and her final weeks before graduation. Quite often Wade accompanied her to various school functions. He frequently spoke of his plans encouraging her to join him. College was the next big step and the University of South Carolina seemed to be the most logical choice for them both.

Dawn had always loved children and had dreamed of teaching in a mountain school some day. The university in Columbia did have a highly credited education department. She knew that her father would approve because he had always insisted that she receive a degree in higher education.

It was an extremely warm springlike day in March when Dawn had a longing to go to her favorite spot on the Edisto campus, the summer house. Daffodils were blooming around the edge of the little house and yellow jasmine was entwined around the branch-like posts. She was really hoping no one was there to disturb her thoughts. After seating herself on one of the benches, she soon found that the warm rays of the sun felt good across her back. It was then that a little robin perched itself on the bannister and began singing a cheerful tune.

"Well, Mr. Robin, I see that you are excited too and welcoming in spring. If you could just talk, and tell me what to do. Why does life have to get so complicated?" contemplated Dawn as she wrestled with decisions that seemed to be demanding attention.

The robin cocked his head toward her as if he really understood her thoughts before flying into the wind-swept sky. Was this the robin's way of telling her that she must be more prayerful about what God would have her do with her life? Where was He leading her? The choice of the same school where Wade would attend could be the turning point in her life. He would probably accept it as a confirmation that she was joining her life with his. "Oh, Lord," she whispered, "please guide me; don't let me make a mistake. I so want to do Your will." It was then that she noticed the sun sinking lower toward the horizon bringing a slight chill in the air.

The last few weeks of school seemed to disappear as quickly as the water evaporated from the hot sand after a spring rain. Graduation from the academy was just a few days away. Excitement filled the air as final plans were made for the big day.

Dawn and Alice were relaxing in their dorm room taking advantage of a few quiet moments to be together before their life at the academy would come to a close.

"Dawn, it's hard to believe that we are finally graduating!" exclaimed Alice as she began to pack up some of her school belongings.

"I know, Alice, and we'll be in college in a few short months and then—'Real World, here we come!'" teased her roommate.

They had become very close friends-almost like sisters-during their years as students at the academy.

Suddenly there was a loud knock on the door.

"Come in," called Alice.

A fellow student opened the door with a serious look on her face and quickly announced, "Alice, Mr. Washburn would like for you to come to his office at once. You have received a telegram from home."

"Really," replied Alice, "did he say what it was about?"

"No, just that it was urgent and for you to come immediately."

Seeing the look of alarm in her friend's eyes, Dawn sprang to her feet and was soon beside Alice giving her a big hug. "Come on, Alice, I'll go with you if you'd like me to," encouraged Dawn with a reassuring tone for her long-time friend.

"Oh, would you please? Something must be terribly wrong at home."

They hurried as quickly as possible to the president's office. After a quick knock on the door, Alice was ushered into Mr. Washburn's office.

"Did you want to see me, Mr. Washburn?" asked Alice trying to catch her breath.

"Yes, Miss Stewart, please sit down," answered the president, as he handed her the telegram from her father.

With her hands shaking, Alice opened it and read: "Your mother extremely ill. Catch train home at once. Pa Pa"

"I'm so sorry, Miss Stewart, we'll make arrangements for you to leave as soon as possible. Was that your friend waiting in the outer office? You will need someone to help you pack quickly, and then we'll get you to the train station."

"Thank you, Sir. Yes, Dawn Randall is with me, and I'm sure that she will do all she can to help."

As soon as she left, she flew into the outer office and into the arms of her best friend who was anxiously waiting to hear the news. "Dawn, it's Mama. She's very sick, and I need to go home now! Will you help me get ready to go?"

"Of course," replied Dawn, "I'm so sorry. What can I do to help?"

"Just help me pack a small valise now, and I'll return as soon as I can for my other things. Oh, Dawn, I don't know if I'll be here for graduation. It really sounds serious."

"I know, but I have already prayed for you and your family. 'God is a very present help in trouble,' you know."

The Rift of Dawn

"I know and thanks, it's so comforting to remember His Word."

In just a few moments, the girls had packed some necessary items and were hurrying down the hall. As they started down the steps to look for her ride to the train station, Alice heard her cousin, Wade, calling her name. "Alice! Alice! Over here, Mr. Washburn has asked me to accompany you to the station with him. Let me have your bag. I am so sorry to hear about Aunt Lillian. Is there anything else that I can do for you?"

"Thank you, Wade, I don't know what I'll find when I get home. Please keep us in your prayers. If I don't get back, you may have to see that my belongings are sent home. Could you do that for me, please?"

"Don't worry at all about it. It's as good as done! Dawn will help me, I'm sure," replied Wade reassuringly.

The horse and buggy wasted no time in getting to the railroad station. "Look," called Wade, "there is your train pulling in now."

Mr. Washburn had been so helpful in making all the arrangements that soon Alice was saying, "Goodbye," and boarding the train.

Alice sat at the window as the train pulled away from the station. She waved one last time to her cousin and Mr. Washburn and wondered what the future held for her.

Meanwhile back at the academy, Dawn waited impatiently in the summer house for Wade's return. Her thoughts wandering back to happier days when she and Alice had started as roommates at the academy with such high hopes and dreams. Dawn did not want to think that maybe they would not finish together. Trying to calm her thoughts, she prayed silently for her friend and her family. She couldn't imagine what it would be like to lose HER mother. "Dear God," she prayed, "I know that you are in control and that You don't make mistakes. Please hold this family in Your loving arms until this storm is passed."

Hearing horses' hooves approaching, Dawn opened her eyes to see Wade getting ready to depart from the buggy and hurry over to where she was waiting. Soon he was there by her side and reached for her hand.

"Alice is on her way home. The train left on time. She is very concerned about what is facing her at home. I assured her that her things would be taken care of here, and she would be in our thoughts and prayers. She really appreciates the fact that you were with her when she got the news," continued Wade as he squeezed Dawn's hand. It was evident that he needed her support now, too. After all, this was part of his family, as well. They then walked silently, each in his own thoughts, but hand in hand back to the dining hall.

Chapter 11

Graduation Day

Graduation Day dawned bright and clear. There was much excitement on the Edisto campus as parents and guests began to arrive.

There had been no more news concerning the condition of Alice's mother. Dawn was anxious to learn any news about Mrs. Stewart from Wade's parents who were to attend the graduation program.

Dawn had been busy all morning packing up all of her and Alice's things in their dorm room. Now she was waiting for her family to arrive. She sat by the window to observe the goings and comings outside. Several people were at the summer house enjoying the spring like morning. As she waited, she lapsed into a pensive mood reflecting upon the many memories that she had had there in the summer house-the sunset encounter with Rawl, quiet moments with Alice, decisive musings with the delightful robin, and the special time with Wade when he gave her the cross pendant that she had worn in the Christmas concert. She was sad to think that these happy times were coming to a close.

At that moment she heard a soft knock on her door. Jumping up, she ran to the door to find her parents and Ken waiting to see her.

"So your big day is finally here! Are you ready?" exclaimed her father.

"More importantly," teased her brother, "Is the world ready for you?"

"I'm ready!" Dawn shouted as she hugged them all.

The chapel was filled with excited parents and other guests. Windows were opened to allow the spring breeze to blow through, providing some relief from the increasing warmth in the room. Dawn and the other graduates filed down the aisle to their reserved places at the front. She smiled at her parents who beamed back at her proudly.

After taking her place, she was briefly saddened as she thought of her best friend, Alice, who was not at her side. News from Wade's parents let her know that the condition of Alice's mother was still very serious even though she was showing some improvement and recognition that Alice was there with her.

"Ladies and Gentlemen, Parents, Faculty Members, Distinguished Guests, and Honored Graduates, we welcome you here for this special occasion," began Mr. Washburn as the audience quieted to give him their full attention. The program continued with the recognition of various certificates and awards. Following several speeches, the moment that they had all been waiting for finally arrived. Each graduate's name was called as he proudly walked across the stage to receive that coveted diploma. A hardy applause resounded following the last person who received his.

It was then time to sing the school's alma mater for the last time as a senior class. Dawn felt a lump in her throat but did her best to sing with enthusiasm.

On the old hillside a dreaming, when the sun is in the west,
When the bird notes are the sweetest and the village is at rest;
When the wind is in the pine trees, and the chapel bell is still,
There is rest for mind and spirit, at this haunt upon the hill.

Tell us not of larger schools, with their greater wealth endowed
For despite their attractions, of our own we still are proud.
Scarce we understand the reason, but the very soul seems dear,
And we always breathe the freer, in this clear, pure atmosphere.

Now the violet is blooming, and I dream the oriole calls,
Now my heart is faint and restless, for familiar paths and halls,
When the heart is only longing, little sympathy it finds,
And I sigh for dear old Edisto, and the wind among the pines.

Chorus:
You may go where'er you please, from the North to southern seas
And you'll find no music sweeter than the wind in old pine trees;
How each restless tho't it stills, how the heart with rapture thrills,
When the green comes back in springtime to the dear old Edisto hills.

The graduates received a standing ovation as they left to depart from these hallowed halls of learning. With mixed emotion, Dawn said, "Goodbye," to her classmates and particularly Wade. It seemed a long time until fall when they would be together again at the university.

Chapter 12

USC

Dear Alice,

    It's hard to believe that I have only one more year here at the university. I have really missed you while you have been at home helping care for your mother during her lengthy illness. I know that you miss her now that she is gone. I'm sure that it must have been difficult for you to assume so many responsibilities. I do admire you for all that you have done for your family. It will be good for you to return to school in the fall. My roommate, Dianne, is sweet, but I have missed our quiet talks and your often unsolicited advice. Just teasing, of course. She has spent much of her time in the study room. This has given Wade and me a lot of time together at the library and walks throughout the campus. He is really pressuring me to join him on the mission field.

    Please pray with me that I am listening to God's voice and not just his. I have learned to love Wade and really do admire his devotion to God's calling for him.

    See, I really do need you and am looking forward to your coming in the fall. Now I must get back to studying for these final exams.

                  Lovingly,
                   Your Friend, Dawn

The Rift of Dawn

After addressing the envelope and placing a stamp in the corner, Dawn left her room quietly to drop the letter in the mail at the campus post office. No sooner had she finished her task when she saw Wade coming toward her.

"Hello there, Miss Letter Writer, who's the lucky recipient of that letter that you just mailed?"

"Just a quick note to your cousin, Alice. I'll be so glad to have her here with us in the fall."

"How about having a soda before study hour begins?"

"Sounds good. These warm afternoons are getting me so sleepy making it difficult to study."

Catching her hand, Wade directed their steps to the campus canteen. After getting each of them a soda, he steered Dawn to a quiet table in the corner.

"Thanks, Wade, this really is refreshing."

"Just like you are," winked Wade. "You really have become very special to me, Dawn, and I would like for us to plan our lives together on the mission field. Have you been praying about this?"

"Yes, Wade, I have, but I want to be sure that God is calling me, too."

Catching her hand again, he looked her straight in the eye and said, "I don't believe that He would be telling me one thing and you another."

"I know, Wade, but I have to be sure. I have always felt that He was calling me to teach in a mountain school. You must give me some space to be still with God. He alone knows what is best for me. I do care about you and what you plan to do with your life, but I can't be pressured into just your plans. Do you understand?"

"Of course, Dawn, I would never do that deliberately. Forgive me if that is what I have been doing. It would never work if God didn't call you, too. It is so hard to let go, but I know you so well. Whatever you do takes all that you have, I just hope that I am in the picture of your life somewhere."

With that thought and the look of apprehension in Wade's eyes, Dawn realized that he had taken a giant step backward because he had always been the more assertive one in their relationship.

"Thank you, Wade, for your patience. This will give me some time this summer to allow God to mold me into a fitting vessel for Him to use with you if this is His will."

With the shadows of the afternoon sun deepening, the young couple started toward their respective dorm rooms, each enveloped in his own thoughts and aspirations. The lengthening shadows of the evening sunlight seemed to permeate the very being of Dawn's inner soul. If she could only be sure...

Life at Four Oaks was thriving with the usual summer planting and activities. Dawn could see that the fields had been planted in cotton and would be white like they were blanketed with snow come harvest time. In the meantime her father spent much of his time in Charleston with Ken who managed their lumber business there.

She had been welcomed and pampered by her mother and Mammy since her arrival home from school. It had been a wonderful relief from the rigors of university life, adjustment to school without her best friend, Alice, and the pressures of Wade to make a decision concerning their life together.

Several weeks had gone by and things had pretty much settled into a normal routine for the returning daughter of the Randall family. The summer days were long and hot here at the Four Oaks Plantation. There were very few cool places available for Dawn to sit and contemplate her future. Since she was usually an early riser, it seemed logical for her to slip out to the garden during the early morning hours to see the sunrise. There was a slight breeze in the air as the golden glow of the sun's rays began to rise slowly above the horizon. Having spent a year in the city where it had been difficult to see a sunrise, Dawn sat motionless for a few moments just taking in the inspiring sight.

"What an awesome God we have!" thought Dawn as she observed the ever-changing view of the rising sun before her ushering in another day.

She was so caught up in the experience of the moment that she almost forgot why she had come to the garden so early. The singing of the early morning birds soon brought her back to reality. Hearing the birds reminded her of the friendly little robin who seemed to try to communicate with her at the summer house back at the academy. "What was it that was so special about that little bird?" Oh, yes, now she remembered as she recalled how it soared above her head into the sky as if to say, 'Keep your thoughts upward!' She must be sure that it was God's voice, even if it were a still small voice, that she must obey.

"What if God were speaking to her through Wade? Could this be possible?" She would have to consider this possibility. It did seem as if the last time she and Wade had discussed their future that she was looking into the face of God and saying, "No!" Bowing her face in her hands she prayed, "Oh God, I can't say, 'No,' any longer. I can't see into the future but You can, so I am trusting You with the decision that life on the mission field with Wade is Your will for both of us." What a weight seemed to be lifted form her heart!

The sunlight warmed her face as it climbed higher above the tree tops. "Yes, this is going to be another scorcher," thought Dawn as she rose to walk back to the house on the hill, but in her heart she knew that it would be a good day.

"Well, hello there, Missy. You sure are up and out early this morning," announced Dawson as he headed toward the barn to take care of the animals. "It already seems warm out here. It's going to be another hot day. Yes, Ma'am, that it is!"

"I think you're right, Dawson. I had some thinking to do and decided that the garden was a good place to do it, and watching the sunrise was an extra bonus," grinned Dawn as she closed the garden gate.

"Your Ma and Mammy are already in the kitchen getting breakfast."

"I can smell that good country ham from here," smiled Dawn. "I sure didn't get that at school. I can hardly wait to sink my teeth into one of Mammy's ham biscuits."

She lingered for a moment on the walk before entering the house. The decision that she had just made was uppermost in her mind, and she knew that her mother would notice her pensive mood as soon as she saw her face. If only she could see Wade and tell him about her prayer. Somehow she felt that he knew because he seemed so certain that this was God's will for both their lives.

"Any ham biscuits left for me?" she called out as the back door closed behind her.

"There you are. I thought I saw you in the garden early this morning. Is everything all right? You have seemed a little quiet lately," questioned her mother.

"Oh, Mother, you know me so well. Oh, how I wish that Wade were here. I have just turned it all over to the Lord out there in the garden. He knows much better than I do what the future holds. I could no longer say 'No,' when I realized that I was saying, 'No,' to God's will. I have said, 'Yes,' to God, and now I'm going to say, 'Yes,' to Wade when I return to school in the fall."

With a knowing glance toward Mammy, Mrs. Randall reached out to her daughter with both arms. "Mammy and I have joined our hearts in prayer for you here in the kitchen. We have sensed the struggle that you were having over the last few months. We have been praying that you would place the final choice in God's hands. Your Father and I like Wade very much and believe that you will make a wonderful team on the mission field."

Breathing a sigh of relief and with tears streaming down her cheeks, Dawn melted into her mother's arms. "It is so good to know that I have yours and Pa Pa's blessing. It isn't going to be easy living so far away from all of you, but I can have real peace and joy only when I go where God leads."

"I have an idea! Would you like to invite Wade here for a weekend before you return to school? There are many things that we need to discuss, and I am sure that Wade will be happy to hear of your decision as soon as possible."

"Oh, could we, Mother? That is a wonderful idea! I'll get a letter in the mail today!" exclaimed Dawn as she reached for one of Mammy's ham biscuits before racing to the writing desk in the parlor to pen a note to Wade.

Chapter 13

Wade's Visit

"Ken, it is so good to have you and Pa Pa here for this special weekend. I do hope that the train is on time," fidgeted Dawn in her seat in the buggy.

"Do try to sit still; Dobbin won't get there any faster with your trying to hurry him along," teased her brother as the horse trotted along the dusty road to the small railroad town nearby.

The sun shone down unusually warm that morning, and there didn't seem to be a breeze anywhere. Dawn almost wished she had decided to wait at home. Maybe it would have been a few degrees cooler inside.

"We are almost there," announced Ken. "Does Wade know that you have made a decision concerning your future together?"

"Oh, he has probably guessed; I just told him that I couldn't wait until fall to see him."

Turning around the next bend, Dawn leaned forward to look for the train. Yes, there it was, on time as usual. A few passengers had already departed from the train, but none of them looked like Wade.

"Do you think that he missed the train, Ken; I don't see him anywhere?"

"If he did, my guess is that he would walk every step of the way to be with you," answered her brother.

At that moment they both saw Wade stepping off the steps of the train and heading in their direction. Dawn rushed into his arms and received a very special kiss and embrace letting her know just how much she had been missed.

Ken politely lingered for a moment by the buggy and then walked over where they were, extending his hand for a hardy handshake with his soon to be brother-in-law.

"It has been a while since I last departed from a train at this station," said Wade, remembering his stay at the academy. "It is good to see you again, Ken," smiled Wade.

After getting his luggage from the porter, Wade joined Dawn and her brother at the buggy, and they were soon on their way back to Four Oaks.

"It was quite a pleasant surprise hearing from you before the fall term. I hope that this means some good news," questioned Wade anxiously as he gave Dawn another hug.

"Yes, I do want to talk with you, Wade, but it will have to wait for my special place in the garden. Mother and Pa Pa are eager to see you, too."

After catching up on the news of Alice and the family, the group's buggy approached the long oak-lined drive toward the large white house on the hill.

A warm Randall welcome awaited Wade as he once again enjoyed the hospitality of Dawn's family. After some time with the usual pleasantries, Mrs. Randall asked Ken to take Wade's things to the guests' bedroom upstairs. She then suggested that the young couple might want to spend some time alone in the garden.

"We'll have dinner in the dining room at three o'clock," she said as she started toward the kitchen to help Mammy with the meal.

"I have some things to do, too, so make yourself at home, Wade. We're glad that you could come," said David Randall as he started down the hall.

"It looks as if your family wants to give us some time to talk. I can hardly wait to hear what you have to say," whispered Wade when they were finally alone.

"Well, you'll have to wait a few more minutes until we go out to the garden. It is really beautiful out there and one of my favorite places in the world."

Catching his hand, Dawn led him out the front door and down the path to the garden. "There is a bench under the grape arbor, and maybe it will be a little cooler there," she explained as the young couple ambled toward the peaceful spot in the garden.

Wade could hardly believe that he was here with her at last. Dawn really did look stunning in a light-blue dress that accented her golden blonde hair. He noticed that she was wearing the pendant cross that he had given her at the academy the day before the Christmas Choral concert. Reflecting upon that memorable occasion, Wade noticed that today, with its hot and humid summertime weather, was quite a contrast to the icy wind that blew through the open gazebo that cold December day.

It really did feel a bit cooler under the shade of the arbor as Dawn motioned for him to sit beside her on the bench.

"Wade, I hardly know where to begin. I have thought of little else since returning home. I have spent much time in prayer seeking God's will for both of our lives. It was recently right here on this bench that I realized I was not just saying 'No' to you, but I was also saying 'No' to God. I am willing to go with you wherever He leads us. I do love you, Wade, with all my heart and am looking forward to our spending our lives together with God."

Reaching for his hand, Dawn realized that he was also reaching for hers, and he held her in his arms for a while. "Oh, Dawn, I was so afraid that you were going to say, 'No' again and finally this time. I just couldn't imagine life without you. With you by my side and being my inspiration, I believe that we can accomplish whatever God would have us do. I thank Him for you every day. I do love you very deeply." With that said Wade kissed her again and held her closely to himself. It was then that she realized just how much she loved Wade and that life with him held some exciting adventures ahead.

The two of them just sat quietly together for a few moments neither of them wanting to break the spell of what they each had just experienced.

Finally, it was Wade who spoke first, "Dawn, there is one thing that I need to do now."

"And what is it that is so urgent?"

"I need to find your father and properly ask his permission to marry you."

"Then, let's go find him!"

Chapter 14

School Again

Returning to school in the fall was filled with promise. Seeing Alice again and realizing that she was really back at school to stay was such a comfort for Dawn. Although they were unable to share a room because of Alice's delay in returning to college life, the two friends spent as much time as they could together. They no longer had the liberty of late night talks much to Dawn's dismay, but she frequently found time to relax with Alice. These times had been good for Alice, also, because it had been difficult adjusting to school and all its demands so soon after her mother's death.

And so the school year progressed with Dawn sharing her time as much as possible with her two best friends, Wade and Alice.

She and Wade were now engaged to be married the following summer. Wedding plans were already underway. There would be a garden wedding at her parents' Four Oaks Plantation. Her mother and Mammy were already busy making her wedding gown and finalizing other plans. This school year just couldn't go by fast enough for her.

While reminiscing about all that had happened, Dawn almost didn't hear the soft knock on her dorm room door. Quietly the door opened and her best friend, Alice, stepped into the room.

The Rift of Dawn

"Got a minute for your best friend?"

"Of course, please come in," announced Dawn as she closed the book that had not held her interest all afternoon. "I am finding it harder and harder to study for these final exams. What about you?"

"I know what you mean. Being away for a few years has made it difficult for me to get back into the routine of studying. And now I keep thinking of your wedding. Just think in a short while you will be Mrs. Wade Stewart, and we will be cousins. It really is exciting! I'm so glad that you have asked me to be your maid of honor. I think the color of my dress, robin's egg blue, will be so pretty in your mother's garden. Everything is going to be just perfect."

"Remember the little cheerful robin in the summer house at the academy that I told you about? He made such an impression on me that I had to include him in some way in the wedding," explained her friend.

"That is so like you, Dawn. You always have a reason for everything that you do even down to the smallest detail. Wade surely is a lucky guy!"

"Oh, no, Alice," replied Dawn very quickly, " I'm the lucky one to be a part of what God is doing in Wade's life."

"Well, both of you are very special to me, and I look forward to seeing how God is going to use you as a team."

Glancing at the clock, Alice observed the lateness of the hour. "I've taken up enough of your time. We had better get back to studying for our finals," remarked Alice as she stood to leave.

After Alice left, the room seemed quieter than ever, as Dawn picked up her study notes for a final review. Alice had been such a good friend, and she had her to thank for getting to know Wade. It was her prayer that Alice would meet someone just as special.

Chapter 15

Wedding Day

Graduation Day finally came! Much to her surprise a box with a dozen red roses arrived at Dawn's door. They were from Wade with a note that read, "Congratulations and best wishes for our future life together! With all my love, Wade."

"He is so thoughtful," reminisced Dawn, recalling other occasions in her life when he had done something special for her.

Her family came to support and congratulate her for her most recent accomplishment. She finally had her coveted diploma in her hands and was looking forward to teaching as well as helping Wade in his work.

Now it was time to focus on wedding plans. Virginia Randall and Mammy had spent many hours making Dawn's wedding gown. It was exquisite in every detail. The bodice was made of Chantilly lace with a sweetheart neckline. It had long sleeves ending in Calla lily points over the wrists. On the full skirt of satin and tulle, an applique of lace flowers outlined in seed pearls ended in a chapel length train. Dawn was sure to be a vision of loveliness on her wedding day.

Invitations had been sent and preparations were being made to have a barbecue celebration following the ceremony.

The Rift of Dawn

The day of Dawn and Wade's wedding finally arrived. Fortunately the day began with the rising of the sun and without a cloud in the sky. As usual Dawn was up with the sun to take one last walk in the garden before the guests arrived that afternoon. Late summer flowers were in bloom; some were twining with ivy around the garden trellis that was to be used as the wedding altar. Folding chairs had been placed on either side of the garden walk among the flowers that had managed to survive the summer heat. Everything seemed to be in place. Quietly Dawn tiptoed back upstairs to take one last look at her dress before the others were awake. How pleased she was with her mother and Mammy's efforts in this endeavor! She knew that it had truly been a labor of love for both of them.

Although Dawn crawled back into bed, there was too much to think about to go back to sleep. It was then that she heard a soft knock on her bedroom door. Before she could arise to answer it, the door opened slowly as her mother peeked in. "So you are awake already, I was hoping to wake you one more time before you become Mrs. Wade Stewart," smiled her mother as she sat on the edge of the four poster bed.

"Oh, I was much too excited to go back to sleep. Is this how you were when you married Pa Pa?" asked her daughter.

"Well, yes and no. I was very much in love with your father, but we were in difficult times then just after the war. We didn't have any money for much of a wedding ceremony. It was a sad time that my father had been killed in the war and was not there to give me away. My mother was still grieving, not only over the loss of Pa Pa, but the lifestyle that she had always known was no more. I was so thankful for your father. He is such a strong person. You are very much like him."

"And I love him dearly. I am so glad that he is going to give me away."

"You always were very special to him from the day that you were born. You were the apple of his eye."

The rest of the morning passed very quickly and soon it was approaching time for the guests to start arriving.

Dawn's bedroom had been a beehive of activity as Mrs. Randall and Mammy helped her get dressed for the wedding. Alice had arrived early that morning to be with her friend on this important day.

Dawn looked absolutely radiant in her wedding gown. She was wearing pearls that belonged to her grandmother. Her blonde hair was in curls that cascaded from the back of a double banded floral hairpiece from which flowed the floor length veil. When Mrs. Randall was satisfied with her daughter's appearance, she gave her one last kiss and hugged her before she started down the curved staircase toward the front hall and outside to the garden.

Alice whispered as she went before her friend toward the garden and the waiting wedding guests, "You look beautiful, and I love you."

Out in the garden, the guest violinist was rendering the wedding music. Even the birds seemed to know that it was time to be quiet. Every guest had been seated and the wedding party was in place by the trellis altar. Wade's steady gaze was on the garden path waiting to see his beloved Dawn. Mr. Randall, with his daughter by his side, began the long walk down the garden path to the smiling groom. Dawn kept her eyes on Wade until she reached the end of the garden walk and then she turned to smile at her mother before reaching for Wade's hand.

Fortunately, the ceremony was brief because the afternoon sun shone down mercilessly on the wedding party and guests. There was some relief under the spreading live oak trees during the barbecue celebration. During this time the young couple had an opportunity to mingle with their guests and receive many best wishes from those attending the festive occasion in the Randall's garden.

Following the cutting of the delicious wedding cake, the newly weds excused themselves to change into traveling clothes for their departure. Because of limited funds and time before seminary classes started, the young couple was combining a honeymoon trip with a search for living arrangements while away at school.

Before joining Wade in his buggy, she stopped to say a quick "Thank you" to her parents followed by a long goodbye hug. After a final wave, the young couple started down the tree-lined drive to begin their new life together.

Chapter 16

Letters

Dear Mother and Pa Pa,

Wade and I are finally settled in our tiny apartment here in the married section of the campus community. Space is very limited here, but we are thankful to have living quarters available so near our classes. Wade has also been asked to preach on Sundays at a nearby church. I do all that I can to help and support him. God has been so good to supply all our needs.

I miss all of you very much and look forward to coming home for the holidays.

Love to you all,
Dawn

Each week a letter arrived at the Randall household and was eagerly read and reread. It was always such a joy for Virginia Randall to hear about the activities of her children. She was already looking ahead and planning for the holidays when her family would be together again. Nothing pleased her more than doing things for her family that she loved dearly.

The lumber business in Charleston was doing well, and David had spent more time at the plantation especially during the time of the cotton harvest. Ken was assuming more of the management of the lumber business so his father could spend more time at home. This pleased Virginia very much because the large house seemed so empty now with Dawn's being married and so far away.

As the Christmas season approached, Mrs. Randall began her usual preparations with the holiday decorations. Smells of evergreens- cedar, pine, and holly- began to fill the house.

"Jennie! Jennie!" called David as he came into the house. "We have another letter from Dawn and Wade. Come into the parlor, and we'll read it together."

Wiping her hands with a towel, Virginia quickly came into the room and joined her husband by the cozy fire. "You read it, David, while I catch my breath."

"Sure, Darling, have a seat here beside me." David quickly opened the envelope and read aloud:

Dear Mother and Pa Pa,

It is very cold here today. Wade went to preach at his church this morning for the first time without me. I have been so very tired recently and not feeling like myself. Wade insisted that I go to the infirmary, and guess what the doctor said? We're going to have a baby! That was a surprise to us. The doctor advised me to rest and curtail my activities.

He was a little concerned because I was anemic and started me on some vitamins and iron tablets. They are helping because I am already feeling some better.

Wade is excited but worried about me. We'll be glad to come home for some TLC from all of you.

Hope you are all well. We can hardly wait to see you. I can almost smell the holiday decorations that I know you are bringing inside for Christmas, Mother. Tell Mammy to start baking some of her special goodies.

Love to you all, Dawn

"David, do you think that it is safe for her to travel here?" questioned Mrs. Randall with a look of concern on her face. "If she doesn't take care of herself, she could lose the baby, you know!"

"Now, Virginia, don't start scaring up trouble. I'm sure that Wade will do what the doctor advises. Just think! We're going to be grandparents!" With that said, he reached over and kissed his wife and gave her a big hug.

The next few weeks seemed to drag by as Virginia Randall made final preparations for Christmas and anticipation of her daughter and son-in-law's return home.

At last the day came when David left to go to the train station to bring the young couple home.

"Here, David," called Virginia as she hurried to the buggy before it began to pull away from the front drive. "Take this shawl to put around Dawn when you come home. There is a chill in the air this morning, and she mustn't get cold."

David, who was always eager to please his wife, took the shawl and laid it beside him on the buggy seat.

"There! There! Jennie, I'm sure that they will come well prepared." After giving her another goodbye kiss, he was on his way.

The morning seemed to drag by with Mrs. Randall's pausing every few minutes to look for their return. Mammy had been busy preparing all of Dawn's favorite foods. Steaming hot cocoa was ready to be poured into mugs and served by the fireplace in the parlor. The cedar and holly garland over the mantel released an aroma of evergreen scent as the warmth of the fire permeated the room.

At last the sound of horses' hooves were heard coming up the long drive toward the house. Dawson soon opened the large oak front doors to welcome home the young couple. David and Wade slowly helped Dawn step down from the buggy. She did appear to be somewhat frail and pale, but nevertheless she managed her usual smile.

"Miz Randall, Dawn and Master Wade is home," called Dawson over his shoulder as he opened the doors wider to let them inside.

The Rift of Dawn

Hurrying into the large entrance hallway, Virginia Randall scooped her daughter into her arms with a warm loving hug.

"Merry Christmas, Mother, it is so good to be home again!" exclaimed Dawn as she melted into her Mother's open arms.

"Come on in by the fire and get warm. Mammy has some hot cocoa ready for you," replied her mother.

At that moment Mammy entered the room with steaming mugs of hot cocoa on a tray. "Welcome home, Honey Chil', Yo' sho has been missed!" announced Mammy with a smile as big as the county on her face.

David and Wade soon joined them after bringing in their luggage and depositing them upstairs in the bedroom. After noticing Wade in the room, Virginia quickly went to his side with a warm welcome. "How was the trip, Wade? Dawn does seem tired and a little pale."

"It was a little long and uncomfortable for her, but I'm sure that she will be fine now that she is back here with all of you."

After a few days of rest, color began to return to Dawn's cheeks, and she appeared to be her usual bubbly self.

Ken arrived home on Christmas Eve to spend a few days with the family. Mrs. Randall was enjoying having everyone under the same roof again. She had tried to keep the celebration rather low-key this year for Dawn's benefit. Even though Dawn tried to be a part of the holiday activities, her mother noticed that she was often sitting by the window with a pensive look on her face.

Finally the day after Christmas, Mrs. Randall took the opportunity to spend some time alone with her daughter. "Dawn, you have seemed a little quiet recently. Is everything all right?" questioned her mother.

With tears in her eyes, she confessed that something did not seem quite right. She was concerned about returning to the rigorous demands of seminary life, but she didn't want to let Wade down.

"Honey, your body is going through a lot of changes now. You need to take care of yourself and this baby. Wade will understand. Why don't we make an appointment with Dr. Stone while you are here-just to ease your mind. I'm sure that Wade would agree. He loves you so."

"Oh, could we, Mother? I don't want to worry Wade unnecessarily."

"Of course, your father can make the arrangements. Now you just relax; we'll take care of everything."

Yes, just being home again did ease her mind somewhat. Her mother always did know what to do.

Chapter 17

Alarming News

"Dawn is in the doctor's office for an unusually long length of time," thought Wade as he sat nervously waiting in the outer office. Virginia realizing his concern reached over and patted his hand. "Try to relax, Wade; Dr. Stone is a wonderful doctor. He delivered Dawn, you know, and has cared for her all of her life. I can assure you that he knows her quite well."

It was then that the nurse asked Wade to come into the examining room where Dawn was. Wade quickly sprang to his feet and in no time was down the hall and into the room where Dawn and Dr. Stone were waiting. When he entered the room, Dawn weakly smiled at him and took his hand as he sat down beside her.

"Mr. Stewart," said the doctor, " I asked you back here to talk with you about Dawn's condition. I am concerned that she is not as strong as I would like for her to be to carry this baby to full term. She is going to need lots of bed rest and as little stress as possible. I don't believe that she should be traveling any long distances until after the baby is born. I am recommending that she stay here with her parents until after her delivery. I can be in touch with her doctor and can be in charge of her care here."

There was a look of apprehension in Wade's eyes as he answered, "She is all that I have, and her health and care mean everything to

The Rift of Dawn

me. Whatever you think is best we will do, Doctor." It was then that Dawn lovingly squeezed his hand to let him know just how much she appreciated his love and concern for her.

With that said, the decision was made for Dawn to remain at Four Oaks when the time came for Wade to return to the seminary.

Dawn and Wade spent some time together by the fire in the parlor discussing their immediate future. "Wade, I am so sorry that I am unable to return with you. Who is going to look after you?"

Catching her hand and giving it a tight squeeze, Wade interrupted her and said with loving concern as he looked into her eyes, "Don't you worry about me; I'll be fine. You just focus on taking care of yourself and our little one. I'll miss you terribly! It will be hard for me to concentrate because I'll be thinking about you every day. Just remember that I will be back before the baby is born, and there will be letters."

To reassure her, he held her in his arms for a few moments. Dawn appeared to relax a little and kissed him tenderly.

The time came for Wade to depart for the train all too quickly for the both of them. David loaded Wade's luggage on the buggy and waited for him to join him. After one last embrace and kiss goodbye, Wade reluctantly climbed into the buggy for the ride to the train station.

Waving goodbye from the porch, Dawn couldn't keep the tears from flowing. It seemed that the next few months would last forever until they could be together again.

Realizing the emotions that her daughter was experiencing, Virginia encouraged her to lie down and rest for the remainder of the afternoon.

The cold winter days at times seemed almost endless for Dawn. She felt that she had read every book on the library shelves-oftentimes just turning the pages with mindless reading. She was really looking forward to spring.

At last the days began to be warmer, Mrs. Randall suggested that an afternoon in the garden, a change of scenery, might just do the trick for her daughter. She had spent many days sitting by the fire making clothes for the baby. Dawn had even learned to knit, making some little sweaters and bootees.

Dawn welcomed the idea of spending some time in the outdoors and, wrapping herself in a warm shawl, walked with Dawson out to the garden. He had arranged a bench in a sunny area and saw that she was comfortable before leaving her to enjoy the afternoon sun. The Yellow Jasmine was blooming as well as some of the early spring bulbs. Just being out in the open brought a smile to Dawn's face and seemed to lift her spirits. At that moment she heard a chirping sound and looked up to see the first robin of the season hopping around on the ground nearby. This wasn't the first time that she remembered a robin had captured her attention. Somehow she felt that everything was going to be all right.

Letters from Wade helped to pass the lonely hours as she waited for his return. Each visit with Dr. Stone was encouraging. He was pleased with her progress. In just a few more weeks she would be holding their precious little one in her arms. She could hardly believe that she would soon be a mother.

The coveted letter finally arrived in the mail! Wade would be coming home on the afternoon train this coming Saturday. It seemed ages since they had been together. Would he recognize her with all the weight she had gained? She couldn't think about that now. She hoped that he would notice the color in her cheeks and that she had gotten the rest that she had so desperately needed.

Wade had only been home for a couple of weeks when Dawn awakened early one morning with beginning contractions. Her mother was called into the room and confirmed that her daughter was in labor. As the pain increased, David hitched up Dobbin to the buggy and went for Dr. Stone.

As Wade and her mother waited anxiously for their return, Dawn began to be more and more in anguish. It was obvious that she was having a difficult labor. Wade held her hand tightly with each contraction, Virginia sponged her forehead with a cool cloth.

The Rift of Dawn

The upstairs bedroom was becoming increasingly warm from the heat and humidity so prominent in the deep South during the summer months.

Finally voices were heard downstairs as Dawson let the doctor and Mr. Randall in. Dr. Stone gave some quick instructions to Mammy and hurried up the stairs to the room where Dawn was about to give birth. Seeing the urgency of the situation, he sent Wade downstairs for Mammy to come right away.

David took Wade into the parlor with him and said, "Let's pray together." The two men knelt beside the sofa and placed the situation in God's hands. They prayed for Dr. Stone to have the wisdom to do what was best and that Dawn would have renewed strength to have a healthy baby. David also prayed for Wade that he would experience peace and calmness at this difficult time.

After what seemed like hours, the sweet sound of a baby's cry could be heard from the upstairs bedroom. A look of relief spread over Wade's face as he jumped to his feet to start up the stairs. Quickly David reached over and caught his arm. "Just give them a little while longer. Dr. Stone will be down with some news as soon as he has finished." Reluctantly, Wade sat back down, but it was obvious that he was very concerned about his wife.

At last the bedroom door opened and Dr. Stone appeared in the hallway and motioned for Wade to come upstairs. Taking two steps at a time, Wade was soon at his side anxious to hear what the doctor had to say.

"Mr. Stewart," said Dr. Stone, "You have a beautiful and healthy baby girl; however, your wife has had a very difficult time during delivery. She is extremely weak and exhausted from her long labor. Because of what she has been through, I believe that it will be risky for her to have any more children. That is something the two of you will have to decide."

"Dr. Stone, I would not do anything to put my wife's health or life in danger. Thank you for all you have done. May I see my wife now?"

"Yes, but she may not be fully awake or aware that you are with her. I have given her a sedative so that she will sleep. Do not stay long as she needs to rest now."

Walking into the room, Wade tiptoed over to Dawn's bedside. She looked extremely weak and pale. Leaning over he kissed her forehead and held her hand tightly. "I love you, Darling. Thank you for our beautiful daughter!" whispered Wade as he sat beside her bed. Dawn opened her eyes briefly with a hint of a smile before closing them again in sleep.

Quietly Wade prayed, "Thank you, Father, for our little daughter. Please spare my wife's life and strengthen her is my prayer."

Wade sat quietly by his wife's bedside studying her pale features carefully. He realized just how close he had come to losing her. It wasn't until Mammy came in sometime later and asked him if he would like to see his daughter that he realized that he had not seen or held his little girl yet. "Yes, Mammy, I would. I have been so concerned about Dawn that I almost forgot about the baby."

Virginia entered the room at that moment and took him through the door into the next room. Guiding him to the bassinet, she showed him the tiny baby girl who was sleeping quietly. "Here is your beautiful little daughter," smiled Mrs. Randall. "She reminds me so much of Dawn when she was born. Have the two of you decided on a name for her?"

"As a matter of fact, we have. We had already decided if we had a boy, the name would be David Wade after Dawn's Pa Pa and me. But if we had a girl, she would be named Dawn Marie after Dawn and my mother."

"And so Dawn Marie it is!" announced the proud grandmother.

As the weeks went by, Dawn slowly regained her strength. Often Wade would take her out into the garden early in the morning before the hot afternoon sun beamed down so heavily through the trees. Some days she insisted on bringing the baby with her so she could enjoy the outdoors, also. Hearing the birds in the overhead trees always brightened Dawn's spirits. It wasn't long before Dawn Marie would open her big blue-green eyes to see what was making the sounds above her. Looking up Dawn noticed at least a half dozen robins chirping away loudly. Gazing into her little daughter's eyes, she announced excitedly, "Those robins, my Precious, are the first sign of spring!" It just seemed natural then for Dawn to call her little daughter, 'My Little Robin.' One day Dawn was sure that she saw her smile at the sound of her new name. And so it was that Dawn affectionately called her daughter, Robin.

Chapter 18

Life on the Mission Field Three Years Later

"It seems that we are always saying 'Goodbye,' Mother," said Dawn, "and this time it will be for four years."

With seminary training behind them, Dawn and Wade had been commissioned to work in the foothills of the Latin American country of Venezuela. All their belongings had been packed and some of them had already been sent to Charleston where they would board a ship for passage to their new home.

Dawn and Wade were already in the buggy ready to go to the nearby train station. Virginia Randall picked up her little granddaughter, Robin, gave her one last hug and kiss, and deposited her onto her mother's lap for the ride to the train station.

Dawn took one last look at the home she loved so much as the buggy started down the tree-lined drive. She wondered what her new life would be like in a different world. With Wade by her side and God directing their lives, she knew that it had to be rewarding. Their future indeed looked bright!

The train ride to Charleston was long and tiring especially for Robin who was not accustomed to sitting still for long periods of time. At last the ordeal was over as the train pulled into the station.

Upon their arrival, Dawn and Wade noticed a flurry of activity happening in this port city. There were people everywhere- in the shops as well as along the streets. Life here in this bustling metropolitan area was quite different from the more tranquil life in the country that had been home for Dawn for so long. It didn't take very long; however, for them to spot Ken and Elizabeth whom he had recently married. Plans had been made to stay overnight with them before leaving early the next morning for South America. Dawn liked her new sister-in-law right away. Elizabeth was very warm and friendly.

They arrived late in the afternoon at the large new house which Ken had built on Cummings Street in downtown Charleston. "Ken, your house is beautiful, and Elizabeth, you have done a wonderful job with your personal touches in decorating it," admired Dawn as they toured the new house. It sat some distance back from the city street. There was a wrought iron fence on the street side and a well-landscaped garden to one side of the house.

After giving her guests time to relax a bit, Elizabeth served a light supper on the circular side porch that overlooked the garden. A breeze coming off the ocean gave some relief from the August heat.

Because they were to be at the dock early the next morning to depart on a ship, Dawn excused herself to put Robin, who had been nodding after a long day of travel, to bed.

Shortly after sunrise the next morning, Ken took the young family to the shipyard to board a ship to their final destination. A cool breeze blew in from the sea and the weather looked favorable for sea travel.

Dawn found herself saying, 'Goodbye' again as they boarded the ship for a new life that would be different from all that was familiar to her. Wade seemed confident and smiled as he waved one last time to his brother-in-law on shore. Robin who was in her father's arms waved with two hands and smiled a big Stewart smile.

Finally they were in their cabin, and Dawn arranged their personal belongings as best she could, so they would feel as comfortable as possible during the time spent on ship.

Wade soon went up on deck and met some of the other passengers. One family had some children that he later introduced to Dawn and Robin. Being with them helped the time to pass faster during their voyage.

The Rift of Dawn

At last the ship arrived at the young couple's destination. Another missionary couple was there to welcome them and show them their new home. After debarking from their ship, they joined their new friends and traveled by donkey and wagon with their possessions to a small village at the foot of the Central Highlands.

Dawn felt comfortable with their new found friends, Carrie and Robert Sims, who were ready to help them adjust to their new lifestyle and become accustomed to the language. The Sims were involved in medical missions with a small clinic there. A small church was already established as well as a tiny mountain school. Wade was needed to pastor the small mission church, and Dawn would teach in the school. There was one other teacher who also served as the administrator.

After a few days of getting settled in their new living quarters, Wade left to survey the area and learn more about the native people that he was to pastor. Robin had a harder time adjusting to her new surroundings. She clung to her mother's skirt most of the morning. Finally exhausted, she lay down for a nap.

Mrs. North, the school's administrator, came by to meet Dawn and discuss some of her new school duties. She was very businesslike in her manner; however, this made Dawn feel more secure in her new position.

As days turned into weeks, the Stewart family became more accustomed to their new home and country. Robin quickly learned some Spanish words and enjoyed the Nanny who looked after her during the school day while her mother was teaching.

Wade's mission church grew rapidly, and Dawn enjoyed teaching in the mission school. In a letter home to her mother, she wrote:

Mother, you know how I felt that God wanted me to teach in a mountain school. Well, it occurred to me recently that I am doing just that. We are living in the foothills of the Central Highlands, and it is beautiful here. I often look out the window at school and admire God's handiwork as I see the beautiful mountain slopes in the distance.

  Robin seems to love it here now. She is learning so much Spanish, I fear we may have to teach her English all over again when we come home.

I hope that you and Pa Pa are well. We miss you very much, but are happy here knowing that we are in God's will. Please continue to pray for us as we pray for all of you.
Your loving daughter,
Dawn

Letters continued to be a welcomed connection with the family back home. Even Robin learned through the letters that the world was larger than the village that was becoming home to her. She often squealed with delight when her mother read letters from her grandmother that she affectionately called 'Grandma Jennie.'

Chapter 19

A Brief Interlude

Wade was very committed to the work that he was doing. He often traveled to nearby villages to share the truths of the Gospel with everyone that he could. He sometimes lost track of time and did not get home until after Robin was in bed. His erratic behavior began to be a concern to Dawn when days would go by, and Robin had not seen her father. She also noticed that Wade seemed thinner and listless. She wondered if he were remembering to eat while he was meeting the needs of others.

One day while at the clinic, Dawn mentioned to Carrie her concerns about Wade's health. She further explained that working such long hours seemed to be affecting his health. Carrie listened intently as Dawn shared these cares with her and then replied, "Dawn, I've noticed that Wade is extremely dedicated to his reason for being here. That is good, but it is also the reason we have furloughs. The spirit is often willing, but the flesh is weak. Getting away for a while helps us to have a new perspective of our mission here. It helps us to realize that we are only one cog in the giant wheel of God's work. It is then that we come back renewed and with understanding that it takes time to build relationships and earn the trust of the people here. Wade needs you to be a support and encourager for him. And I believe that you are. He loves you and Robin so very much."

Dawn often thought about Carrie's advice and decided on a strategy hoping that it would help to maintain a balance in Wade's life of concern for the village people as well as life with his family.

As usual, Wade came home appearing tired and drained. She met him at the door with a loving kiss and encouraged him to relax while she reheated the meal that she had prepared earlier, which included some of his favorite foods.

Calling him to the table, Dawn sat with him, sipping a glass of iced tea, while he ate. Trying not to be condescending, she calmly stated, "Wade, you have been working so very hard lately trying to reach as many of the mountain people as you can. I have an idea that, I believe, Robin will really enjoy. Since there is no school tomorrow, why don't the three of us take a picnic lunch up the mountain by a beautiful waterfall that I recently discovered. You deserve a day of rest, and I'm sure that Robin would love it. She asked the other day, 'When is my Pa Pa coming home?'"

"Did she really? I have been neglecting you two a bit, haven't I? That's a good idea; let's do it!"

"Not neglecting us, just doing what God has called you here to do."

"It's just that I can't bear the thought that someone on these mountains has never heard the good news that Jesus loves them and died for them."

"And I so admire your dedication. I just want you to renew your strength so you can tell each one. Now you go and get some rest while I pack a lunch so we can get an early start in the morning."

"Sounds like fun! What would I do without you?"

Giving him a hug from behind, Dawn smiled and answered, "That's something I don't want you to find out."

The sun rose the next morning without a cloud in the sky. "A perfect day for a family outing!" thought Dawn as she finished packing a basket of everything that she thought they would need for a delightful picnic together.

Robin was so excited to learn of the plans for the day. As the little family started on the trail up the mountainside, Robin was laughing all the way perched on her father's shoulders. Dawn was pleased to see that Wade seemed more relaxed and that he had entered into the fun she had planned for the day.

Before long they were singing some little songs that Robin knew as they trudged up the hillside toward the waterfall.

"It isn't much farther now," encouraged Dawn, "I think I can hear the waterfall, and it does seem to be a little cooler."

The vegetation began to change as they neared the damper area of the waterfall. "There it is, Mama, there it is!" squealed Robin as she pointed ahead.

As soon as they reached the falls, Wade slipped off his and Robin's shoes and waded out into the small pool at the foot of the falls. The water was cool and refreshing since it had come downstream from the higher elevation.

Dawn sat back against a large rock and savored the moment as she watched her husband and daughter enjoying being out in this beautiful natural setting. It had been some time since she had seen Wade so at ease.

The fun filled morning went by quickly and soon it was time for lunch. Dawn spread a gingham tablecloth over a nearby flat rock and placed the lunch she had prepared on the makeshift table. She even picked a few wildflowers to make it more appealing and placed them in the center of the table.

"Lunch is ready, you two. Are you hungry?"

"Starving!" called back Wade as he placed his little daughter on his shoulders again and ran over where Dawn was waiting with Robin laughing all the way. It was obvious that she was enjoying this special time with her father.

After lunch, Robin who was tired after her romp in the water, settled her head back onto her mother's lap and promptly fell sleep. Dawn was enjoying this quiet time with her husband by her side and almost fell asleep herself. Instead she was determined to stay awake and savor the time that she had with him alone which was becoming all too rare.

Wade sat with his arm around his wife and shared with her some of the goals he had concerning his work and ways that she could

The Rift of Dawn

help accomplish them. This really pleased Dawn because sometime she felt that they were there on two totally different missions.

The afternoon passed all too quickly for Dawn. Noticing that the sun began to lower behind the mountain, Wade said reluctantly, "This has been great, Dawn, but it will be getting dark soon. We had best gather our things and start back down the mountain."

And so they did, but Dawn knew that she would keep the memory of that day in her heart for a long time.

Chapter 20

Ten Years Later

While observing her daughter, who had already grown into a young teen, Dawn wondered where the time had gone. She and Wade had discussed several times the possibility of allowing Robin to finish school at Edisto Academy where they had been educated. They had many fond memories of their experiences as students there themselves. Finally, they had decided that after the completion of this year, they would be returning home for another furlough. This would be the ideal time to make arrangements for her to attend the academy and stay with her grandparents as her guardians.

Wade continued to work diligently among the native people. He now was preaching at two other small churches higher in the mountains. Oftentimes he would go with Robert to visit the sick who were unable to come to the clinic. It wasn't unusual for him to sit by a sick one's bedside holding a hand, praying, and speaking words of comfort for hours. Thus he neglected his own health, not getting the nourishment and rest that his own body needed. It was almost as if he were more obsessed with the needs and concerns of others rather than himself. No amount of coaxing to slow down from Dawn or their missionary friends, Robert and Carrie, seemed to have any long term effect on him.

The Rift of Dawn

Quite a few of the members in Wade's mission church had become sick with a mysterious illness. Even though Dawn encouraged him to rest more, he seemed compelled to visit each one with words of comfort. Robert and Carrie were doing all that they could with their limited supplies to alleviate the suffering; however, in spite of all they could do each village was losing some of its people.

Each night as Wade came home exhausted, Dawn could see the extra burden that he was experiencing knowing he was losing some dear friends and not being able to do anything. Some evenings he cried in Dawn's arms as he related to her the events of the day. They often prayed together that God would intervene and heal the village of this devastating disease; nevertheless, Wade continued to keep up his daily vigilance.

The mission school was closed early for the season in hopes of slowing down the spread of the disease thus giving Dawn time on her hands. She helped Carrie when she could at the clinic. It was after an extremely busy morning when they noticed Robert hurrying toward the building with two natives behind him carrying someone.

Dawn gasped when she realized their burden was Wade. He looked so pale and appeared to be unconscious as he was brought through the open door into the clinic. Robert quickly called to his wife to ready the examining table and other needed supplies. Carrie encouraged Dawn to wait in the outer office while they diagnosed the situation.

Finally Robert came to Dawn and, as calmly as he could, told her that Wade in his weakened condition had contracted the mysterious fever and that the prognosis did not look good. Together they prayed and put Wade's condition in God's hands.

All through the rest of the afternoon and evening everything possible was done to bring down the fever, but to no avail. Dawn refused to leave his bedside hoping against hope that he would rally long enough to recognize that she was there by his side. Robin was allowed to come in and sit with her mother for a while. Dawn gave her daughter a hug and assured her that her Pa Pa loved her very much. Then they said a prayer together. She wanted her to know that God had a plan that would ultimately be the best for all of them.

It became more and more difficult for Robin to stay awake during the slowly passing midnight hours. Carrie offered to take her into their living quarters which were adjacent to the clinic. Reluctantly she left her mother to get some much needed sleep.

Robert and Carrie sat with Dawn throughout the early morning hours. Carrie and Dawn took turns sponging Wade with cool compresses to try to bring down the fever.

Finally just before dawn, Robert noticed that Wade's breathing was becoming more and more labored. Dawn could see that he was becoming increasingly concerned over Wade's deteriorating condition, and, as with the others, there was little else that he could do but pray.

Realizing the gravity of the situation, he caught Dawn's hand and said trying to console her, "Dawn, you should be comforted to know that often Wade stood by the bedside of each one who had reached this stage of the illness and eased their anxiety as they passed from this life to the next. Because of his faithfulness by each one's side, we could see a look of peace on each face as each one breathed his last breath. And now you are being just as faithful to him. 'He has fought a good fight, he has kept the faith, and has finished his course.'

"You must believe this, Dawn, and let him go peacefully. Because you are left, God still has a purpose for your life, and He is not finished with you yet."

And so with the coming of a new day, Dawn saw that Wade had entered into his new life that would be eternal.

Arrangements were made as quickly as possible for Dawn and Robin, along with Wade's body, to board a ship to return to the states. News had been sent to the family back home and plans made for Ken and Elizabeth to meet them on their arrival in Charleston. Because their coming furlough was just a few months away, Dawn had already started packing some of their things. What had been expected to be a joyous time of coming home to spend time with family turned into the saddest day of her life.

The mission board had granted her an early furlough and would discuss with her when she was ready to make a decision concerning her future.

While on ship, Dawn, after a restless night, went up on deck before Robin awoke and witnessed the sunrise over the ocean. Today the sea was calm and the rising sun was beautiful as it reflected over the water. As she stood looking out over the sea, the early morning breeze blew against her face. She could not help but be reminded of their last voyage when Wade was by her side sharing with her his hopes and dreams of their work in South America. He seemed so filled with life and promise to fulfill the mission to which he was so dedicated.

With tears streaming down her cheeks, she whispered a prayer:

"Dear God, My heart is broken, and I can't see your plan now. Fill this void in my life with your love and grant unto me your peace as I trust you to put the pieces of my life back together again, so that I can be a fit vessel for your use. Help me to realize that no matter how devastating my circumstances seem at the moment that you are still in control. Lord, I commit my future into your hands. In Jesus' precious name I pray. Amen"

At the close of her prayer, Dawn felt a wonderful sense of peace about her that brought a calmness to her spirit and let her know that she had nothing to fear.

Chapter 21

Back Home Again

Being home again and in the presence of a loving family somewhat eased the pain that Dawn had been feeling. She was so grateful for their help in preparations for Wade's memorial service and burial. It had been so painful relating the whole experience to Wade's parents and other family members. She could see the heartache on his mother's face because she had lost a dear son. She tried to share with them all the wonderful things that he had done while on the mission field. Even though his life had been cut short, he had been obedient to God's call.

The following weeks seemed to be a blur to Dawn as she was in a daze over all that had happened in such a short time. Her dear friend, Alice, had stayed over a few days after the service and did her best to comfort Dawn. Her mother and Mammy took Robin under their wing and gave Dawn some time to spend with her dearest friend. She and Alice spent many hours talking in the garden and often crying together. Alice always seemed to know how to listen and say the most encouraging words. Dawn really treasured their friendship.

And so it was that weeks turned into months as Dawn began to realize that it was time to make some final decisions concerning Robin's schooling and her plans to return to the mission field. It was difficult to return to the academy where she and Wade had spent many happy times, but she needed to take Robin and do all

The Rift of Dawn

that was necessary for her enrollment there. She did enjoy showing her daughter the dormitory where she had lived for several years, also the summer house where she had experienced the cheerful little robin that spring. Robin smiled when hearing that story again and how her mother had chosen to affectionately call her Robin because of that experience.

It was while they were making the arrangements for Robin to begin school in the fall term that Dawn learned that there would be an Edisto School Reunion at that time. All the former students and faculty would be invited to return for a special time of fellowship. This would be the first one in the school's history. It would be exciting to renew old acquaintances, but she wasn't sure if she were ready for that with Wade's death so fresh on her mind. Maybe she would attend if her good friend, Alice, came also.

A few weeks later a letter arrived in the mail from Alice about the reunion encouraging her to attend. Her mother agreed that she should go believing that renewing happy memories would help to lift her spirits. Arrangements were made to meet Alice at the train station so that they could attend together. There was a crispness in the fall air which seemed to rejuvenate Dawn's spirits, and she actually looked forward to spending time with Alice and seeing some of her old friends and classmates.

A banner welcoming all the new students as well as the former ones stretched across the entrance to the academy. Riding through the entrance brought back memories of the first time that she and Alice had arrived to begin their stay as dormitory students. She was so in hopes that Robin's experiences at the academy would be just as delightful as hers had been.

Some of the classmates who had heard of Wade's death expressed their sympathies to Dawn and Robin. Although she appreciated their concern, it reminded her of the deep sorrow that she had experienced. Being in familiar happy surroundings, she had temporarily forgotten the ordeal of recent months. Because of the change in her mood, this seemed like a good time to excuse herself and help Robin to get her things arranged in her room.

"Alice, Robin needs me to help her in her dorm room. I'll meet you later in the chapel for the afternoon program."

The Rift of Dawn

"Sure, Dawn, I'll wait for you in the lobby just before three o'clock," replied Alice as she turned to greet another classmate.

Back in the dorm room Dawn and Robin enjoyed some mother-daughter time together arranging her belongings in the room. Even though they had not had an opportunity to meet yet, it was obvious that Robin's roommate had arrived because unopened boxes and a trunk were already in the room.

Seeing the excitement in her daughter's face, Dawn reminisced about the time when she first arrived at the academy. "Robin, I know that you are going to love it here. This place has so many wonderful memories for me."

"I already like it here, Mama, and who knows I just might meet my future husband here like you did," said Robin with a twinkle in her eye.

"Well, let's don't rush that. I was a little older than you are now when I met your father. I'll be satisfied for you to concentrate on just your studies for a while."

Noticing that time was slipping away quickly, Dawn commented to her daughter, "It's almost time for your orientation meeting in the dining room, and I must meet Alice at the chapel. It is time for us to go, but I'll see you again before I leave."

With that said they went their separate ways- Robin to begin her new experiences at the academy and Dawn to renew old acquaintances from her past-encounters that held a myriad of special memories for her.

Stopping to speak with a few friends along the way made Dawn a few minutes late in meeting with Alice at the chapel.

"There you are," called out Alice as she recognized Dawn coming toward her. "Did you get everything settled for Robin?"

"Almost. She'll enjoy getting the rest in order when her roommate gets there. I just hope that she will be as good a friend as you have been to me."

"Speaking of friends, you will never guess who I just saw in the dining hall! He was getting everything arranged for the student orientation meeting. Remember Rawl Manning? He is back here on the faculty in the art department. He remembers fondly his brief tenure here during our senior year.

"He joined the army shortly after finishing college and fought in the Spanish American conflict. He has recently retired as a colonel.

The Rift of Dawn

Because of his leadership abilities he is being considered to take Dr. Washburn's place as president when he retires at the end of this school year."

"Really! Imagine that, Colonel Rawl Manning returning to Edisto Academy!" exclaimed a very surprised Dawn.

"He will probably be free following the orientation meeting if you would like to see him," suggested Alice smiling broadly.

"Oh, no, Rawl Manning is in my past and that's where he needs to stay. That was just a school girl crush that I had back then. Life has a way of maturing us, doesn't it?"

"If you say so...we had better take our seats. The program is about to start."

After completing all the legal requirements for her parents to become Robin's guardians, Dawn felt comfortable leaving her to go for a re-evaluation meeting with the mission board in Richmond. It seemed that she could adjust to her loss more readily by staying busy. Plans were made for her to do a series of speaking engagements throughout the state to encourage more people in mission careers. And so the next few months were busy with travel. She found that meeting so many people who were genuinely interested in seeking God's will for their lives in a missions' career to be tiring but very rewarding.

Chapter 22

The Portrait

Life at the academy had settled into a steady routine of classes, athletics, and social events as well as religious activities. Robin and her roommate, Sarah Bivens, enjoyed sharing a room together. They seemed to have a lot in common and were even in some of the same classes. They both had some natural artistic abilities and had elected to take Professor Manning's beginning art class together.

On days when the weather was nice, they would set up their easels near the summer house and experiment with the fall colors in an Indian summer landscape.

Professor Manning often stressed to the class that they observe carefully and paint what their eye saw. The girls laughed about this emphasis when they observed luckily a fluke in nature and incorporated it into their painting. Almost always their instructor would notice it and question them about it. It was always fun to tease and remind him that they were only doing what he had taught them in class, and that was to paint what the eye had observed.

And so an interesting comradery developed among them as their skills began to show promise under his excellent tutelage. It was not unusual for him to join his students outside on campus and lend a hand in improving their work. It was always a thrill for Robin when

The Rift of Dawn

he stopped and admired her work. She learned a lot with this one on one instruction.

Over the years Rawl had become an accomplished portrait painter, and the school had commissioned him to do a painting of the retiring Dr. Washburn to be hung in the entrance of the administration building. The portrait also became an excellent teaching tool as the students observed the progress toward completion.

Robin became so fascinated with his work that she often talked with her grandmother about it. Seeing her granddaughter's continuing interest, Virginia Randall had an idea that she discussed with her husband.

"David, what do you think about our getting Robin's art teacher to do a portrait of her wearing the dress that Dawn wore to her sixteenth birthday party when she met Wade? I'm sure that dress is still in my trunk and will probably just fit Robin now. And let's keep it a surprise for her mother. This will be a reminder of a happier time in her life. She will soon be leaving again for the mission field, so we need to get started on it right away."

"I like it! You always have the best ideas," agreed David as he pulled his wife to himself and gave her a kiss on the cheek.

Seeing how much it pleased her husband, Virginia replied, "Good! I'll go ahead and make the arrangements after I talk with Robin. She will be coming home soon for a break. The hard part will be keeping it a secret from her mother."

Robin liked the idea and was eager to see the dress her mother wore when she met her father. She was fascinated to hear about the original dress of her grandmother's that Sherman's men had destroyed.

"Let's get the trunk down and let me try on the dress. May we Grandma Jennie?" questioned Robin excitedly.

The trunk had been stored away for some time, but when they opened it up, the dress appeared to be as it was when it was packed away. Hurriedly Robin tried it on and was surprised to find that it needed only a few alterations.

Virginia Randall began right away to make the necessary adjustments. It wasn't long before the dress was ready for a fitting. Soon Robin was standing in front of the full length mirror admiring the reflection that she saw before her.

Taken aback, Virginia could hardly believe her eyes! She was viewing an almost identical replica of her daughter years ago when the dress was first worn.

"Robin, I can hardly believe how much you resemble your mother when she was your age. She is going to be so pleased with this surprise portrait."

Following the completion of Dr. Washburn's portrait, Rawl began the painting of the Randall's granddaughter wearing her mother's dress that she had worn at her sixteenth birthday party celebration many years ago.

At first it was difficult to find times when their schedules would coincide. The art studio became a common meeting place as the work progressed. Because the history of the dress was part of the reason for the portrait, the face and hands could not be added to a pre-painted torso as was customary with an itinerant artist. It would take longer to complete. Occasionally the Randalls would visit the studio to approve of the work in progress. Thus a warm friendship developed as time went by. On days when Dawn was away, the Randalls would invite Rawl to dinner to spend time with the family and give him an opportunity to get to know his subject better.

Robin decided that she wanted to wait until the painting was finished before seeing it. This would let her experience the full impact of viewing it in its entirety as her mother would when it was completed, and she would view it for the first time.

Anticipation mounted as the portrait neared completion. Rawl insisted that Robin see his finished work while it was still at his studio. He, too, wanted to see her reaction when she viewed it for the first time.

Finally giving in to his insistence, she agreed to meet him in the art room before it was transported to her grandparents' home. After a soft knock on his door, she heard a friendly voice say, "Come in." There standing beside the finished product, Rawl, with his familiar dashing smile, motioned for her to come and view the image on the canvas.

The Rift of Dawn

Not quite knowing what to expect, Robin walked quietly over where the waiting artist stood. There in a life-like pose on the canvas was a full-length likeness of herself.

She stood speechless for a moment as she admired the beautiful yellow organdy dress that had been her mother's. Rawl had captured the softness of the creamy folds of the skirt in a picturesque way. At last she looked at her face with the rays of light bringing out the golden color of her hair. It was at that moment that she noticed that Rawl had painted her eyes a deep mahogany brown. Her eyes were almost a turquoise blue like her father's.

Could her eyes be playing tricks on her? It was almost like peering into her own mother's eyes. She was sure that Rawl had never met her mother with her unusual eyes; yet there they were staring into her own. An uncanny feeling permeated her entire being.

After several moments of silence, Rawl could wait no longer for a response and asked, "Well, what do you think?"

"Professor Manning, it is breath-taking! I can hardly believe that it is me. You have done a fine job! My grandmother will be so pleased."

"Why thank you, Miss Stewart, I'm glad that you approve. I was not sure of how you felt because I saw a hint of a puzzled look on your face a moment ago, didn't I?" questioned Rawl.

"Yes, you did. You see, I was remembering how you have always stressed with your classes that we should study our subject carefully and paint what we see. I noticed that you have painted me with deep brown eyes and mine are definitely not brown; they're greenish blue."

Caught completely by surprise, Rawl Manning had an embarrassed look on his countenance when he realized he HAD painted what he had seen, but it was on the face of someone in his distant past. Why did Robin remind him so much of the girl with the expressive brown eyes that he met long ago in the summer house right here at the academy?

Picking up his palette that still held the greenish blue pigment and reaching for the paint brush, he attempted to correct his mistake. Quickly reaching for his hand, Robin cried out, "Oh no, don't change it. The girl in the picture looks just like my mother,

The Rift of Dawn

Dawn Randall Stewart. She has wonderful dark brown eyes just like that!"

"So Dawn Randall is your mother! I knew that there was some resemblance between you and someone I had known in the past. Wasn't she a student here at the academy some time ago?"

"Yes, sir, she was. She loved it here, and this is where she and my father, Wade Stewart, became such good friends. Because this school held such fond memories for the both of them, they wanted me to attend school here, also. You see, they were missionaries in South America until my father's untimely death last year. He died from a mysterious illness that was spreading throughout the villages there. My mother will be returning soon to continue working in the mountain village school. That is why my grandmother wanted the portrait finished before she left," explained Robin.

With a pensive look on his face, Rawl commented, "Yes, I do remember your mother. She had the most expressive brown eyes that I have ever seen. We even commented once about the possibility of my painting her likeness one day. I must admit you really do favor your mother."

"Thank you, sir, my grandmother tells me that I do, also."

And so in reality the painting had become a portrait of Robin's mother when she was a young girl.

Chapter 23

The Unveiling

Because Robin's grades were acceptable for a quarterly home visit, she had selected the week before her mother would leave for South America to be home when the painting was unveiled for her mother to see.

The portrait had been hung at the landing of the curved stairway in the Randall's spacious entrance hall. It had been carefully veiled until the appointed time for Dawn to view it.

Since the relationship of Rawl and the Randalls had grown into a warm friendship over the past few months, Virginia invited him to have dinner with the family and be there for the unveiling of the portrait. He then could experience with them the reaction upon Dawn's face when she viewed for the first time the likeness of her daughter on canvas.

Not wanting to intrude on a private family affair, Rawl reluctantly accepted the invitation but only after David and Virginia's insistence.

Dawn arrived home exhausted after a month long schedule of speaking engagements ready for a rest. Shortly after her homecoming, she learned of the plans surrounding the mysteriously veiled painting in the stairwell in the Randall's home.

Robin's excitement about the surprise event they had planned soon lifted her spirits tremendously. It was very tempting to peek behind the veiled curtain on the stairs, but she had promised Robin that she wouldn't.

When she was told that it was a painting done by Robin's art instructor, Rawl Manning, and that he was coming for dinner and the unveiling, Dawn became even more apprehensive. "How long had it been since she had seen him? Would he even remember her? She was no longer the youthful girl that he had encountered in the summer house years ago. And what was that Alice had said about his being in the war?" So many thoughts and questions whirled through her mind.

The following morning she selected a lavender voile dress to wear and pulled her hair back into a netted chignon. Looking into the full length mirror in her room, she noticed that the years had been kind to her appearance even though they had torn at her heart.

Glancing at the clock in the hall, she observed that it was nearing the 3 o'clock dinner hour. Soon Rawl would be arriving at the Randall home. She had been surprised to learn that this was not his first visit here. What else had they not told her? She wondered . . .

Hearing the sound of horses' hooves approaching the house brought a sudden stop to her daydreaming. "He's here! He's here!" called out Robin as she ran to the front door.

Mrs. Randall was close behind her ready to welcome their esteemed guest. Following the sound of the large brass knocker on the oak double door to the Randall home, Virginia opened the door and said smiling, "Please come in, Col. Manning, we're so glad that you could come."

"Thank you, Mrs. Randall, it is all my pleasure. Has Mrs. Stewart seen the painting yet?"

"Oh, no, Robin has insisted on waiting until you arrive. We will have dinner first and afterwards let her see the surprise."

"Splendid! And where is the lady in question?"

"Come this way, Professor Manning. Mama is here in the parlor," called out Robin excitedly.

Dawn was sitting by the window in a large winged back chair. The afternoon sun shining behind her through the lace paneled curtain brought out the highlights in her hair that had been neatly brushed to the back of her neck. Reaching out her hand, Dawn smiled as he came near to greet her.

"So you're the mysterious lady with the deep brown mahogany eyes," smiled Rawl as he grasped her hand with a hardy handshake.

Not quite understanding his comment, she had a questioning look on her face.

Realizing that he had almost given the surprise away, he quickly tried to cover his mistake. "I have just recently learned that you- whose very expressive eyes left a lasting impression on me- are Robin's mother," clarified Rawl.

"Thank you, Col. Manning. I'm surprised that you remembered our encounter at the summer house so long ago," acknowledged Dawn.

"Please call me Rawl!" commanded the strikingly handsome house guest, "now that we are no longer in the student-teacher category."

"I shall, and please call me Dawn seeing that Miss Randall is no longer appropriate," smiled Dawn as she stood to enter the dining room.

Virginia motioned for them to sit on the opposite side of the table across from Robin. It was then that Rawl politely pulled out the dining room chair for Dawn to be seated.

David Randall joined the family as they sat down for dinner. A lighthearted atmosphere filled the room as the meal was served. The family enjoyed hearing about the many travels that Rawl had experienced while serving in the military. Most of them had been during peaceful times. He had a way of making them all sound exciting and, if possible, funny and entertaining. Seeing Dawn laugh as he talked reminded him of the girl that he remembered in the summer house so long ago. It was good for the rest of the family to see her enjoying the conversation also.

Mammy cleared away the dinner plates in readiness for the dessert. "Who would like some homemade apple pie?"

After the dessert was served, Rawl commented, "This pie is really delicious, Mrs. Randall! Are these apples from your orchard here?"

"Yes, they are. As a matter of fact, there is an interesting story about how they came to be a part of our orchard. My father was fighting with the regiment in Virginia during the war and came upon this apple tree in someone's field. Being hungry he was glad to find some ripe apples on it. He really liked the taste of this particular apple and sent the seeds back home in a letter. The seeds were planted and luckily they survived, giving us the apple trees that we have today. We have really tried to take good care of them because, as you know, he did not return from the battle that was later fought there. It has become the last thing that he did for us back here at home. I'm glad that you like the pie. It is one of our family's favorites, also," explained Virginia. "Would anyone like to have another piece?"

"No, thank you, Mrs. Randall, the meal was delicious!" announced Rawl.

"Then let's go into the hall for Mama to see the painting!" exclaimed Robin who was eager to see her mother's response to the surprise. The others were in agreement and retired from the dining room into the entrance hall to view the painting.

At last it was time for Dawn to see the portrait as it was unveiled. All eyes were on her to see her reaction. Slowly David released the covering to show the full length image that was beautifully framed and displayed at the top of the landing of the curved stairway.

Dawn could hardly believe her eyes. She had no idea that the painting was of herself wearing the dress she wore many years ago at her sixteenth birthday celebration.

Finally she said, "How were you able to do this when you didn't attend the party years ago?"

Quickly Robin spoke up, "Oh, Mama, Professor Manning painted me wearing your dress. It was Grandma Jennie's and my surprise for you. Do you like it?"

"Yes, I do! I do!" answered her mother. "It certainly brings back many fond memories for me."

"It was I who painted the deep brown mahogany eyes on the girl in the painting instead of Robin's beautiful turquoise blue ones. She so reminded me of you as I remembered your lovely very expressive eyes that seemed to go with the brown ribbon on your dress. It was Robin who would not let me correct my mistake," explained Rawl.

Stepping back to admire it once more, Dawn spoke softly, "Thank you all. This means so much to me. The memory of that night will always live in my heart."

Later that evening after Rawl had departed and she was left alone with her thoughts in the parlor, Dawn pondered, "Is it possible that after all these years, he still remembers our encounter at sunset in the summer house?"

Chapter 24

Leaving Again

The following few days were spent in packing, shipping her belongings, and preparing to return to the mission field. Robin had already returned to school. It was a little harder for Dawn to leave this time because it was her first time without Wade going with her. Leaving Robin was a little easier knowing her parents were looking after her.

Also she would be under Rawl's close supervision while at the academy. Robin appeared to be totally relaxed in his presence. She was pleased with all that he had taught her daughter in the art department there at the academy. She had not been aware that Robin was gifted in that area. Maybe she would pursue a career in art.

David had chosen to accompany his daughter to Charleston. The train ride there would give the two of them some time together. He wanted to reassure her that Robin would be well taken care of and that they would keep in touch with letters. He thought that it would also give Dawn an opportunity to share any concerns with him that she still might have. Even so, it was difficult for him to watch her return to South America alone for the first time without Wade.

While in Charleston she visited with her brother and his family for a few days before her departure on ship. Ken and Elizabeth's two lively boys, Jack and Little John, kept her from dwelling too much on the fact that she was returning without Wade by her side. She was looking forward to seeing Robert and Carrie again as well as her dear village friends. Robert and Carrie had taken her under their wing from the beginning and had always been there when she needed them. She knew that they would be there to fill the void that she was sure to feel when she returned without her beloved Wade.

There was much work left to do there and staying busy would be good for her, she surmised.

She was not sure what emotions would resurface when she returned to the place where she and Wade had spent most of their married life together. All these reminders would surely cause the sadness of his unexpected death to reoccur. What the future held for her only time would tell. . .

Chapter 25

The Storm

Summers in the south were usually hot and humid, and this year proved to be no different. Quite often Rawl sought relief from the heat and his rigorous duties as Edisto Academy president by riding out to the Randall's Four Oaks farm. He insisted on helping in any way that he could with the work while David was in Charleston. As a result, he became a frequent visitor to the Randall household much to the delight of Dawson who was slowing down considerably because of age.

Electrical storms were not uncommon during the summer months particularly in the month of August. Rawl was aware of these late afternoon thunderstorms and decided to ride out to the plantation to see if everything was all right knowing that Fridays were Mrs. Randall's day to come into town for supplies.

He found Mammy nervously pacing the floor in the kitchen. "Thank Gawd, you'se come, Mast' Rawl. These late August storms sceers me somethin' fierce. Robin has gone out looking fer her littl' lamb, and only the Good Lawd knows where Dawson is," declared Mammy.

"Now, now, you just calm down, Mammy, I'll go find Robin. The wind is getting up, and the storm is about to reach us. You get something ready for Robin to eat when we get back," called Rawl

The Rift of Dawn

as he started down the back steps thinking this would give her something to occupy her hands and mind while he was out looking for Robin and the lamb.

He hurried out to the barn and searched in the nearby fields before he finally found Robin in the edge of the woods near the ripening cotton fields. He sent her back to the safety of the house while he looked farther for the lamb. The soft bleating of the tiny lamb drew his attention to the edge of one of the cotton fields. Shivering from fright the little animal huddled between two rows of cotton. Quickly he gathered the scared little creature in his hands. Plodding through the rich, black fields almost as black as the oncoming storm with the helpless lamb in his big strong arms, Rawl started back toward the large white house on the hill. Even though it was only five o'clock in the afternoon, the sky was so dark that it seemed as if a giant hand had pulled across the sky big threatening clouds blackening out the endless field of blue of only a short time ago. These late August storms usually brought with them loud crashes of thunder and sharp streaks of lightning.

He hurried back to the house because Robin and Mammy were left alone with the exception of Dawson and a few more hired workers, who were just as afraid as Mammy and surely more afraid than Robin, who appeared not to be afraid of anything. Everything was still and quiet except for the soft bleating of the tiny hungry lamb shivering from the chill of the oncoming storm.

A sudden bolt of lightning flashed down from the sky straight toward the earth followed by a crash of thunder which roared across the fields as if it were an echo of the cannon's blast of the advancing Yankee troops of yesteryear. The entire plantation was alighted for a moment as if the west side of the world was afire. It felt as if all the powers of the universe had come down in this one powerful stroke leaving all as quiet and still as it was before.

The tiny lamb shivered again seeming to sense an unforeseen danger in the atmosphere. Large drops of rain began to fall, splashing upon the dust covered cotton bolls and seeping into the black thirsty earth.

Coming into a clearing, Rawl was horrified to behold the sight before him. The west side of the Randall house was on fire apparently ignited by the bolt of lightning witnessed earlier. Black puffs

The Rift of Dawn

of billowing smoke were leaping upward from the roof. Racing toward the back door he found Mammy almost in hysterics and Robin trying to comfort her. Quickly he placed the trembling lamb in Robin's arms and sent them to Mammy's cabin out back so that he could survey the damage. Racing up the steps two at a time, he soon found the bedrooms on the west wing filled with smoke. As he turned to descend the stairs, he momentarily paused to see the portrait on the top of the landing. Briefly his mind remembered the day when it was hung and the look of delight on Dawn's face when she first gazed upon it. It had given him such satisfaction knowing she was so pleased.

Oh how he wanted to save the painting, but smoke was beginning to descend the stairs and he knew that his life was in danger if he didn't soon escape outside. Turning again to the stairwell, his eyes glanced into Virginia and David's bedroom. There beside the open window was a small lady's trunk with a curved lid. Thinking that it probably held some family treasured keepsakes, he quickly ran to it and flung it out the open window toward the shrubbery below. Too much smoke was beginning to fill the room to retrieve anything else so he raced toward the hall and down the stairs.

Everywhere he looked as he rushed toward the door was a reminder of the family who lived here. He wanted to salvage something else, but time was limited. His eyes fell on the silver tea service on the walnut sideboard in the dining room. "It probably has been in the family for years," he thought. Hastily Rawl clutched it in his hands and escaped out the front door.

Rain came down in torrents as he bounded down the steps and around the corner of the house to check on Robin and Mammy. The fate of the Randall home was now in God's hands as the downpour continued to soak the top of the house and pour into the gapping hole that had already burned through the roof. The heart of pine sills and rafters were a ready fuel for the blaze. Much of the upper floor was in ruins as was the side of the house that had received the bulk of the lightning bolt as it traveled to the ground. The deluge of rain was a blessing as it began to squelch the roaring flames.

Soaking wet from the downpour, Rawl soon entered Mammy's cabin and found her and Robin staring out the window not believing what they saw. He found a place to put down the tea service before going into the room to join them to observe the seemingly hopeless situation outside. It appeared, however, that the rains were causing the flames to smolder leaving black silhouetted studs standing ghostly against the sky on the second floor.

Each of them stood motionless immersed in his own thoughts as they stared toward the blackening ruins. It was Robin who broke the silence first. "Grandma Jennie should be home by now. She must have been caught out in this storm. I do hope that she is all right."

"Yas, suh, Mast' Rawl, she do go into town on Fridays to bring back supplies that we needs. She's always home 'fore dark. What a sight fo' her to see. . ." trailed Mammy as she turned to view the disastrous scene across the way.

Startled by the possibility of more forthcoming danger, Rawl quickly started to the doorway. The brunt of the storm appeared to be over now; just a gentle rain was falling. Noticing movement in the barn, he hurried over to find Dawson and the workers who had been in the fields. He quickly explained the situation and left Dawson to look after Mammy and Robin. He also encouraged them to salvage what they could from the smoldering house and to retrieve the trunk that he had thrown from the upstairs window onto the bushes below.

Mounting his horse in a flash, Rawl started down the tree arched drive to the main road. He hadn't traveled far toward town before he saw a sight that would forever remain etched in his mind. There was the overturned buggy with Virginia Randall thrown into the ditch beside it. Springing down from his horse, he felt for a pulse, but to no avail.

Apparently she had died instantly with a broken neck. This may have been a divine blessing because she surely would have been paralyzed had she survived.

Immediately his thoughts were racing, "Could that earlier powerful stroke of lightning have spooked the horse and caused it to run away?" He needed to continue into town to find the coroner and wire David and Ken in Charleston the devastating news of the events of the day.

Before leaving he whispered a prayer for each family member as each one heard the news of these two tragedies. His heart went out to Dawn so far from home and this new loss so soon after that of her husband.

Racing into town, he quickly notified the coroner of the situation and the general vicinity of the accident and hurried to wire the family in Charleston the heartbreaking news. And now he had the inevitable task of delivering the distressing news to Robin and Mammy back at the farm. In his heart he wondered just how much one family could take.

Recalling the biblical truth that God's grace is all sufficient, he knew that the strong faith of this family would see them through.

Chapter 26

A Needed Trip Home

Because of the distance and the time required to make arrangements to return home so soon after the beginning of her new assignment, Dawn was unable to get home in time for her mother's funeral. Rawl had arranged for Robin to stay at the academy with the house mother who was already at work getting the dormitory rooms ready for the fall term. Mammy and Dawson had stayed at Four Oaks and salvaged what they could of the Randall's belongings following the memorial service of Virginia Randall.

The remainder of the Randall family had returned to Charleston to wait for Dawn to arrive from South America. They had decided to wait until Dawn returned home to discuss the final outcome of the Four Oaks Plantation. David Randall had little desire to rebuild and return to a place he could no longer call home with his beloved wife not being there. It was as if something of himself had died with her.

At last the ship arrived bringing Dawn back to her homeland where so much of her former life was missing. Elizabeth and Ken met her at the pier with loving arms. None of this had seemed real until now when she saw the sadness in their eyes.

"Welcome home, Dawn," expressed her sister-in-law as she gave her a big hug. "We are so glad that you are here. Your father needs to see you."

"How is Pa Pa?" asked his daughter as she searched their faces for some hope that he was coping with the tragedies.

"He has been weakened by all that has happened," spoke up Ken, "but without Mama, I'm not sure if he has the will to go on. Your being here should make the difference."

The remainder of the trip to Ken's home was spent in relating to Dawn how strong and helpful Rawl had been through it all. "He contacted the authorities and all of us family members making sure that everyone was settled before he returned to the academy. We can never thank him enough for all that he did for our family throughout these multiple emergencies," said Ken.

"Yes, we have much for which to be grateful where Colonel Manning is concerned," expressed Dawn. "He is a very caring person and very cable in responding during a crisis."

After arriving at Ken and Elizabeth's spacious Charleston home and depositing her things in the upstairs guest bedroom, Dawn went into the parlor where her father was sitting solemnly beside the window. It broke her heart to see him sitting there with drooping shoulders looking years older than when she last saw him. She walked to his chair and dropped to her knees beside him.

"Pa Pa, I am so sorry," she said as she buried her head in his lap.

He placed his hand on her head and patted her hair, but could not express what was in his heart. It was moments before either of them spoke. "I wish that I could have been here, Pa Pa. This has been too much for you to bear alone." With that comment he caught her hand and squeezed it. There seemed to be a slight smile on his face. At last he said, "Your mother always said that I was the strong one in the family, but if the truth were known, it was she who was the rock of our family."

"Oh no, Pa Pa, it was the rock of her faith and that is what will see us through now. You must believe that because that is what she would want us to do."

The following morning Dawn, Ken, and their father boarded the train to return to their Four Oaks farm to survey the damage of the fire and decide what was best for the family to do.

Seeing the blackened ruins where once had stood the stately form of the Randall's two story mansion was almost more than Dawn could fathom. Only the front facade of their spacious home remained with parts of the front two rooms and stairwell escaping the flames. Stepping into the front hall she peered up the stairs to see the charred remains of her portrait still precariously clinging to the wall on one side. She allowed herself a brief moment of reflection when she recalled the day when her mother had arranged for it to be there. She had seemed so pleased to bring this joy into her daughter's life. She also remembered the part that Robin and Rawl had played in the surprise and how he seemed to be right at home there with her family that day.

Feeling a hand on her shoulder brought her back to the moment and the reality of the life she was now facing. "Life has a way of getting right up next to us, don't it, Miz Dawn?"

Turning around to see a familiar face she replied, "Oh Mammy, what are we going to do without her?"

"We'll miss her terrible, but I'se goin' to keep on leaning on the One who will never leave us or forsake us," answered the elderly woman who was filled with years of wisdom that had come from a close walk with the Lord throughout her life.

"Yes, Mammy, yes. That is all we can do now," and she was folded into Mammy's loving arms.

The next few days were spent in going through what had been retrieved from the remains of the Randall's belongings after the fire and discussing as a family what to do with the plantation. David was not interested in rebuilding and with his health failing, he was unable to manage the farm alone. Since Ken's business kept him in Charleston most of the time, it just was not practical to continue farming at Four Oaks.

Mammy and Dawson had relatives in the North who were encouraging them to come and live with them. Because of their advancing age, this seemed to be the most sensible choice to make where they were concerned.

After final decisions had been made concerning the Four Oaks farm, as well as feeling satisfied that all the people involved were properly settled in their new locations, Dawn realized that the time had come for her to see Rawl and thank him for all that he had done for her family.

Once again she was unexpectedly enveloped in a situation with Rawl. Where could all of this be leading...?

Chapter 27

An Encounter with Rawl

With the fall term at the academy ready to begin, Robin was temporarily settled at school. Dawn, at first having arrived back at Edisto Academy, spent some time with her daughter before arranging a meeting with Rawl. Feeling confidant that Robin was adjusting to the trauma she had just experienced, Dawn left her daughter and started toward the president's office on the first floor of the building. After stepping into the outer office, she was welcomed by the receptionist. "Please have a seat, Mrs. Stewart, and I will tell Col. Manning that you are here."

"Thank you," said Dawn as she sat in one of the leather chairs beside the door. It felt strange to be here, knowing that Rawl's name was on the door as president of the academy. She expected to see him come through the chorus door for a rehearsal as he had done so many times years ago. It didn't seem possible that so many years had passed and so much had happened.

It was then that the door opened and Rawl came toward her extending his hand in a gesture of a warm greeting. "Hello, Dawn, it is good to see you again. Won't you come into my office?"

"Please sit down," he said and motioned to a chair across from his desk. "I want to express to you my heart felt sympathy for all you and your family have experienced recently." After seating herself, Dawn began, "Thank you. I just had to come to see you personally, Col. Manning, to thank..."

"Please excuse me for interrupting, but the last time we were together, if I remember correctly, we were on a first name basis. I see no reason to change that now."

"Of course, Rawl," as she continued, "I wanted to come on behalf of my family to let you know how much we appreciate what you did on the day of the two tragedies. We will be forever grateful to you for your quick response and concern during the unforeseen events of that day. I have been told in detail by several family members of your quick thinking and actions. It had to have been divine providence that brought you to the farm that day."

"I did nothing that one friend would not have done for another. You see my frequent visits to your parents' place became a peaceful retreat for me as an escape from the constant demands here at the school. And your mother and Mammy amply repaid me for anything that I did with delicious home cooked meals," responded Rawl once again setting her at ease which seemed to be an attribute of his. "Now that we have balanced the scales," he said with a wink, "what are your plans now?"

"After much family discussion and weighing the pros and cons, we have decided not to rebuild at Four Oaks since there is no one to continue the farming. My father will remain with Ken, my brother, in Charleston. Mammy and Dawson have gone to be with relatives in the North. Robin is settled here at school."

"And what about you?" questioned Rawl intently.

"I feel that I am needed here because of Robin and the care of my father, but I'll discuss my assignment in South America with the mission board next week. My heart is torn between these two places that I love dearly."

"My heart goes out to you, Dawn, as once again your world has been turned upside down. I have thought of you often since that day of the storm, and I have a proposition that I would like for you to consider," suggested Rawl as he leaned across the desk toward her.

Dawn looked up to meet his piercing gaze and wondered what he was about to offer.

"For some time now I have been considering a new position in our theology department to encourage and help interested mission field candidates to know first hand what this type career would involve. You have had first hand experience in this area and a compassion for people in foreign places. You have just said that you feel needed here because of family responsibilities. Realizing that the home that you knew is gone, you would have a place to live here with the faculty and would be near Robin which I'm sure is your first concern. I don't expect you to make a decision today because it will take some time to work out the details even from our perspective. Please give it some thought and prayer as you discuss this with the mission board, and I'm sure there needs to be some closure in South America. Your work could begin here next semester."

Dawn sat quietly for a moment as she contemplated what she had just heard. "I had no idea what you were going to say, but I didn't expect this. Once again I am amazed at how God works and His timing is always perfect. I had felt that my work on the mission field had been completed because there is such a pull here; however, I was at a loss concerning what I would do and where we would live. My appointment next week with the mission committee is to discuss possibly a new assignment since they are aware of my circumstances here. I believe that I am qualified to fill the position that you just described. I would like to discuss this with them. May I give them the information that you have just shared with me?"

"Certainly! I will be glad to discuss with them the outline of the course with input from them to make sure that it accomplishes the purpose for which it is designed."

Standing to leave, Dawn extended her hand to Rawl and said, "Now I see what my family was talking about. You are always ready to do what is needed to alleviate an uncertain situation. I came here to thank you for what you have already done, and find myself looking forward to the future and what God has in store for me here."

"'God does work in mysterious ways; His wonders to perform,'" commented Rawl.

"Oh, how I love those words of William Cowper, especially the last line of his poem... 'God is His own Interpreter, And He will make it plain,'" interrupted Dawn.

"How true that is!" responded Rawl.

"Please keep me informed of the outcome of your visit to Richmond. I am confidant that the school board here will approve your position on our faculty based on my recommendation," continued Rawl as he started toward the door to see her out.

Chapter 28

Transition

The following months were busy ones for Dawn as she met her appointment with the mission board in Richmond. After explaining her situation and the proposition that Rawl had offered, they were in agreement with her plans to teach at the academy and were willing to assist with the curriculum. She finally felt at peace concerning her life at this point and would leave the results in God's capable hands.

It was with mixed emotions that she returned to the mission field for closure there. She worked with her successor at the mountain school to insure a smooth transition for the children. Seeing some of the children that she had taught and how they had grown both physically and spirituality was a comfort to her. She approved very much of the teacher who would be taking her place.

Knowing that there was nothing further that she could do at the school, she needed to see her good friends, Robert and Carrie. Spending time with them helped with her healing process because they had known Wade so well.

At last she would be leaving the following day to return home to stay. Dawn felt that she needed one last quiet time at the place near the waterfall where she, Wade, and Robin had spent that restful day together. Carrie understood and encouraged her to go, but quickly reminded her to leave early because nightfall came soon after the sun dropped behind the towering mountains.

Dawn changed into some comfortable clothes and shoes for mountain hiking and started up the path. It appeared to be somewhat overgrown but was familiar enough that she did not lose her way. Before long, she could hear the splashing of the water falling over the ledge of the rocky cliff above her. The air was cool and refreshing as she looked for a spot to sit and rest awhile.

Many memories came flooding back into her mind. She could almost see Wade splashing in the little pool at the base of the falls as he played with his little daughter. The flat rock across the way still looked inviting and ready for another family to enjoy a picnic there.

As Dawn sat drinking in the atmosphere of the beautiful natural surroundings, she silently thanked God for the opportunity He had given her to be a part of the work He had sent them there to do. She missed Wade terribly and could almost sense his presence there with her. Remembering Carrie's warning to leave before sundown, she reluctantly stood up to leave.

The shadows were lengthening around her as she started back down the trail to the village. Coming to a clearing along the path, Dawn noticed a beautiful cloud with a silver lining. Bright rays of the setting sun were shining over the top edge and reaching out as if into eternity. It was so awe inspiring that she stopped a moment to gaze upon it. It was so unusual that she felt as if she were looking at the underneath side of Heaven with just a hint of its beauty and splendor escaping over the edge of the cloud.

It was almost as if she could hear Wade say, "Oh, Dawn, I CAN see over here on this side, and it is beautiful! There is no way that you can imagine it, but don't be in such a hurry to come. God has much left for you to do on Earth. I see His plan for you, and it is wonderful!"

It was then that she saw the red setting sun at the bottom of the cloud with a bright glowing path leading behind the cloud.

She mediated a moment upon this extraordinary experience and wondered what God had in store for her during the remainder of her life.

She really wanted to linger a while longer, but realized that night fall was approaching fast. So she quickly hurried down the trail to the village and a final evening spent with Robert and Carrie.

After a tearful goodbye with her friends the following day, she returned home in time for Christmas with her family. Ken and Elizabeth invited Dawn and Robin to spend the holidays with them and David in their home in Charleston. It was good for the family to be in new surroundings because Virginia Randall was sorely missed.

Charleston was gayly decorated for the holidays with lighted candles and fresh greenery everywhere. The excitement surrounding Ken and Elizabeth's two lively sons kept them from feeling too sad. Elizabeth served a delicious dinner, and carols were sung around the open fireplace. Dawn was beginning to sense the true spirit of Christmas and thought to herself, "It's good to be home!"

Chapter 29

A New Year Begins

The new year began crisp and cold as Dawn and Robin returned to the academy. Robin was excited to have her mother with her to stay this time. The academy was to become their home at least for now.

Hearing the chatter of returning students after the long Christmas break reminded Dawn of days gone by when she was reunited with Alice, Wade, and others who shared their holiday experiences.

Robin soon recognized the return of her roommate and other friends. After a quick hug and parting wave to her mother, she hurried over to them.

Dawn realized now that it was time to put her best foot forward and begin her new life here at the school she so loved. First, she needed to stop by Rawl's office to pick up her agenda and get her room assignment. Not seeing anyone in the outer office, she knocked softly on his door. Suddenly she heard footsteps coming from the other hall behind her. Turning she was surprised to see Rawl with that familiar smile coming toward her.

"Welcome back," he greeted. "I just saw Robin down the hall, and she said that you were headed this way. Come into my office. I have everything ready for you."

The Rift of Dawn

After they were comfortably seated, he hesitated a moment before talking about school work, to ask about her family and their Christmas holidays. She, in turn, asked about his before discussing the semester's work. After making the necessary explanations, they went down the hall to her classroom.

"Here is your classroom, Dawn. My secretary, Miss Culler, will be glad to help you with any supplies that you need and in any other way that she can. And I am sorry about adding on the extra Spanish classes to your work load. It was, as I explained, unexpected that our former teacher was unable to return for this semester. This should be no problem with your having spoken the language for a number of years. We appreciate your being so willing to accept that extra responsibility. May I wish you a very successful first term with us. I am very glad to have you on our staff."

"Thank you, Rawl, I must say you have done all that you could to make my transition here satisfactory in every way."

"You're most welcome, Dawn. Remember supper is at five o'clock. The faculty still sits together at their regular place. I look forward to seeing you then. Have a great afternoon," said Rawl as he touched her hand before leaving.

After Rawl left, she took a few moments to explore her room. Walking over to the window that overlooked the front campus, she was pleasantly surprised to see that the summer house was just a short distance from her window. Even though this January afternoon was brisk with a little wind, she could see that it was filled with students renewing their friendships. It was interesting that young people did not notice the cold just as she didn't the day that Wade met her there to give her the cross pendant.

She wondered if the robins were just as cheerful and friendly as the little one she had encountered years ago. Reflecting for a moment she thought, "Have any students pondered any life changing decisions as I did there at my favorite spot on the campus?" As she continued down Memory Lane, she could still see Rawl with his easel capturing the sunset on that early fall afternoon. "I wonder if he ever has time to do that anymore," said Dawn to herself as she sat down at her desk to look over her class roll.

The new class was small as was expected this first year; however, her Spanish class was large since a foreign language was required for all students. There would be some advanced classes to fill her schedule, too. She would also be helping another teacher as housemother since she would be living on campus. Looking at her full schedule, she hoped there would be some time left for Robin that is, if Robin would have time for her.

After planning the first day's lessons, she glanced at the clock on the wall and noticed that it was almost five o'clock. She had meant to go back to her quarters, freshen up a bit, and see Robin a few minutes before supper. "Oh, well, that will have to wait." She closed her books and left papers neatly stacked on the center of her desk. She closed her classroom door softly and went to the dining hall.

The custom of the students' having free choice of seating the first day back was still in force so Dawn was not sure where Robin was sitting. Instead of searching for her, she went straight to the faculty table. She did not immediately see Rawl, so she took a seat next to the other housemother, the only other familiar face nearby.

They had finished eating when Rawl appeared and sat at the head of the table. He immediately apologized for his tardiness explaining something about a new student's late arrival. He inquired if everyone had met Dawn, the new faculty member, before quietly bowing his head to say Grace.

Most of the students as well as some of the faculty left the dining hall. When Dawn excused herself to leave with the others, Rawl motioned for her to stay a bit longer. She moved nearer where he was sitting to hear his comments.

"How was your afternoon? Did you find everything that you needed?" inquired the ever attentive Rawl.

"Oh, yes, quite well. Your secretary had done a good job making everything available. My room is very nice and well equipped. Thank you again," answered Dawn with a smile.

"That's good! Just let me know if you find that you need anything else. I do plan to have a brief meeting in the chapel to introduce you to the student body. It will be at seven o'clock. I'll see you then. Please sit down near the front."

"I'll be glad to," said Dawn, "I'll see you then," as she stood to leave.

After freshening up a bit she went to the opposite end of the hallway looking for Robin. She was not in her dorm room. "She is probably out with her friends before the class assignments begin," thought Dawn as she started back to the chapel. Following Rawl's directions, she sat on the side front row. The students soon began to fill the room chattering and laughing as they came.

The meeting was brief as Rawl had promised. He welcomed the students and staff back saying that he hoped everyone had enjoyed the holidays. He announced that a few new students had enrolled for the spring semester. Then he asked Dawn to stand as he introduced her as a new faculty member explaining briefly her position on the staff. After a few more announcements the meeting then closed with the singing of the alma mater and a prayer. He encouraged the students to go to bed early so as to be refreshed for their early morning classes.

Chapter 30

An Unexpected Afternoon

Dawn was a little nervous as she began her first day of classes at Edisto Academy, but later she was pleased that the morning went so well. The previous teacher had done a super job with the beginning Spanish classes. She was glad, however, to have a lunch break.

Robin stopped briefly at the faculty table to inquire about her mother's morning. "The first day's classes have gotten off to a good start," answered her mother. "How was your morning?"

"Great! I've even heard some positive comments from some of the students about their new Spanish teacher," winked Robin as she turned to find her place at lunch.

The others at the staff table were interested in her first morning's activities making her feel very quickly a part of the group. Rawl was not among those present and no one explained why. Apparently he was often absent tending to school business that took him elsewhere.

The mission orientation class met right after lunch. It was small as was expected with only eight students. After meeting with them, she felt that they were truly called of God into some type of mission service either at home or abroad.

After becoming acquainted with them and hearing of their individual goals, the remainder of the time was spent in explaining the syllabus of the course. The first part of the semester would be spent on an in depth study of how Jesus called His disciples and their responses. They would also study in detail Paul's early missionary journeys. The last half of the course would be sharing practical applications of activities on the field. This would be an opportunity to share some of her real life experiences.

The positive response of these students had her energized at the close of the class. She felt assured that God had led Rawl to incorporate this course in the school's curriculum. One of the purposes of this chartered denominational school was to provide Christian training for its students. She really felt good to be a part of this endeavor.

The remainder of the afternoon was spent in lesson plans and her duties as housemother in one of the dormitory halls. She also tried to spend some time with Robin each day as their schedules allowed.

As the weeks turned into months Dawn was pleased with the progress her students made especially the mission orientation group. She could see them growing spiritually as the semester neared the half-way mark. And then spring fever hit! The warm days brought more of the students out-of-doors. The summer house was always filled with those who were trying to briefly escape from their rigorous studies. She couldn't much blame them because there were afternoons when she longed to be outside, also.

The third quarter was coming to a close, and those students who had earned a brief trip home because of satisfactory grade performance were making plans to depart. Robin had been granted special permission to spend time with Sarah, her roommate, at her home since the academy was temporarily Robin's home, and she had no other home to visit.

With just a limited number of students remaining at the academy, Dawn found that she had time on her hands even in the capacity of housemother.

Realizing that Dawn had been confined to the campus since her return in January, Rawl approached her when Robin left and asked if she would be interested in riding with him out to the Four Oaks farm on Saturday. Her eyes brightened with the thought of going home, but then she realized it would not be the same.

"How kind of you, Rawl, I would love to," said Dawn not believing what she was hearing. "But can you afford to leave the campus even for a few hours?"

"Surely the school will survive for a few hours without us. You are entitled to some time away from the campus, too. In the past, when I visited your parent's farm, I always came back refreshed and better equipped to tackle whatever was facing me. I'll ask Miss Culler to get the kitchen staff to make us a lunch, and we'll have a small picnic. How does that sound?"

"Wonderful!" announced Dawn trying not to show too much excitement in anticipating the event. It had been so long since she had done something on the spur of the moment just for fun.

Dawn arose the next morning really looking forward to the trip to her parents' farm with Rawl. She quickly looked through her closet for an appropriate outfit to wear.

The spring days were usually warm, but sometimes there was a cool breeze in the air. At last she decided to wear her light blue cotton skirt and a tailored white blouse. Just in case it was cooler in the garden, she grabbed her white shawl with the pink embroidered flowers around the edges. She brushed her hair back into a netted chignon and placed a small blue ribbon at the back. Glancing in her dresser mirror she hoped that she was suitably dressed for the occasion.

She hurried down the hall and out to the gazebo where Rawl had said he would meet her with the buggy. With a limited number of students still on campus, she was relieved to find the summer house empty. She didn't relish explaining to anyone why she was leaving the campus with the president.

In just a few moments, Dawn heard the sound of horses' hooves approaching. Rawl pulled on the reins and could be heard commanding, "Whoa!" to his horse. In a flash he was down from the buggy and walking over where Dawn was waiting. Removing his hat and with a sweeping bow, he said with his usual handsome grin, "Good morning, Fair Lady, would you like a ride into the country?"

Dawn quickly replied, "Why thank you, kind Sir. I would love it."

Not appearing cautious at all, Rawl reached for her hand in his flamboyant style and assisted her into his buggy. As soon as she was settled, he climbed into the seat beside her and gave the horse the command to pull back into the drive. In no time at all, the horse trotted through the entrance gates and out onto the main road leading to the Four Oaks farm.

Rawl was the first to speak. "You look quite lovely today, Dawn. I do hope that you will enjoy a few hours away from the academy."

"Thank you! I wasn't quite sure what to wear or what to expect, returning to a home that is no longer there," she replied as she looked off into the distance at nothing in particular.

"Well, let me tell you what you can expect. A time to just relax and enjoy a spring afternoon with a friend. I have brought my sketch pad in case I see something that looks interesting to draw while you are relaxing."

Dawn found Rawl to be an interesting conversationalist for the remainder of their ride that went past the little railroad town and out the country road that led to her parents' farm. The weather was pleasant for a spring day and beckoned them to be outside enjoying it.

Just ahead of them was the familiar tree lined drive that she had traveled down so many times before. Everything looked the same until she saw that there was nothing left facing the four oak trees at the end of the drive. Apparently her father or Ken had instructed someone to remove what was left of the front two rooms and the entrance hall that was still standing after the fire. In the distance she saw Mammy's cabin as well as the barn and some of the other outbuildings.

Looking around at all that was missing made her realize just how much her life had changed over the last few years. It was then that tears began to well up in her eyes. She blinked several times to keep them from spilling over and rolling down her cheeks. She felt that if she ever started crying she would never stop, and Rawl was trying so hard to make this a pleasant day for her.

After tethering his horse and giving it a pat, rubbing his hand down the horse's mane, Rawl reached for Dawn's hand to help her down from her seat in the buggy. Then he picked up his sketch pad and the picnic basket before starting toward the garden path just ahead.

"Oh, I almost forgot," he said turning back to the buggy and reaching to get something from the floor. "We may need this blanket to sit on," said Rawl.

"Here let me help you carry something," responded Dawn taking the blanket. "The bench in the garden may still be there," added Dawn as she led him between the two century plants at the entrance to the garden.

A number of weeds had begun to sprout up here and there among the spring bulbs that were blooming. The dogwood trees were white with blossoms. Dawn saw the remains of her mother's handiwork throughout the area. At last they turned the bend on the trail and there indeed was the bench. The very same bench that she had sat on years before and made her decision to marry Wade. Now, she felt that it was time to make some new memories.

Chapter 31

Deep Thoughts Revealed

"Here is the bench, Rawl, we can use it for a make shift picnic table and spread the blanket here," explained Dawn motioning to a grassy spot beside it.

After a leisurely lunch, Rawl took out his sketch pad and began to draw while Dawn gathered up what was left of the lunch and placed it in the basket. She sat on the bench quietly for a few minutes with a faraway look in her eye.

"A penny for your thoughts," said Rawl as if to say, "Let me come where you are."

Reluctantly, Dawn began to share what was on her mind as she had been watching him sketch. "I was just thinking about all that has happened to us since we first met at the academy years ago. You are such an intriguing person, Rawl. Why did you never marry?"

"Several reasons, I suppose. I joined the militia and was in the Spanish American conflict shortly after college. Then I continued in the military until I retired recently. Moving around as much as I did with no permanent home was no kind of life for a wife and family. But probably the main reason was I never found that special someone."

"And who might she be?" inquired Dawn encouraging him to continue.

Glancing up at her from his drawing and then pausing momentarily, he slowly responded, "Well, frankly, I never really made a list, but I would say someone who has her priorities in order, meaning putting God first in her life and seeking to do His will above her own, having similar interests as mine, someone who would laugh with me as well as let me share her hurts. In short, I guess I am looking for a soul mate." With a quick smile that could capture any girl's heart without even trying, he ended his requirements by saying, "And someone who could put up with me on a never ending basis."

"You don't expect much," teased Dawn, "I can understand why you never found her."

Putting down his pencil and pad, Rawl looked up into Dawn's eyes that he had grown to love dearly and said very seriously, "Oh, but I think that I have..." And then pausing momentarily, he continued, "Dawn, you have all these qualities that I admire in a woman...all but maybe the last one." He said with a twinkle in his eye. "Only time will tell there!"

Baring his soul to her, he then continued, "I have seen your faith grow stronger with each adversity that you have faced. You have a loyalty to God first and then your family. You so willingly accepted the position at the academy that I offered you, knowing the potential impact it could have on future generations. I have also appreciated your interest in my painting which, I believe, is a God given talent. And you have a sense of humor that keeps me on my toes! So you see that you are that special someone who has all of these qualities that I admire." Even Rawl was surprised to realize that he had actually expressed his true feelings aloud to this one person who had become so very special to him and deep in his heart he was growing to love.

There was an awkward silence for a moment while Dawn collected her thoughts. Was she dreaming or had Rawl just said what she thought she had heard? Finally she responded by saying, "I have always had the upmost respect and regard for you, Rawl, because you were always so much in command of any situation. I am overwhelmed to learn that you have feelings like these for me."

"My purpose for bringing you here today was to give back to you some of the pleasure that you have given so many people including myself. Life has dealt you some rather harsh blows, Dawn, and you deserve better. With your permission, I'd like for us to continue building on these kinds of experiences and making some new memories together."

"I'd like that too," smiled Dawn.

At last the veil that seemed to separate them at times had been completely removed.

"Now, would you like to see what I found interesting enough to sketch today?"

"Of course, I was wondering if I would have to wait for another unveiling," teased Dawn as she stood to look at the pad.

Turning the page so she could see it, there was a penciled drawing of herself sitting on the bench before him. Rawl tore it from the pad and handed it to her while he waited for her comments.

"It really does look like me, Rawl. May I keep it to remember this day?"

"It's yours, that's why I did it."

Realizing the lateness of the hour, Rawl suggested that it was time to start back to the academy. It was then that Dawn spoke up, "Wait, Rawl, before we go, could we take a quick walk back to Mammy's cabin and take a look in the barn? It would mean so much to me."

"Sure, Dawn, a quick walk might do us good. That was a very filling lunch," replied Rawl as he reached for her hand.

Dawn became excited as once again she walked the short distance to the cabin thus bringing back many memories of bygone days.

When Dawn peered inside the doorway, Mammy's cabin seemed lonely and forlorn. Everything was so empty without her dear friend there inside. She was suddenly glad that Rawl was with her.

"Maybe this wasn't such a good idea," replied Dawn sadly starting toward the door of the cabin. "Let's take a last look at the barn before we go."

In just a few moments Dawn and Rawl were entering the shade of the barn. There inside was a lingering smell of the barn animals that were sheltered there for so long.

Dawn almost expected to see Dawson coming from one of the stalls. For a brief moment Dawn felt as if nothing had changed. After quickly looking into each of the areas, she finally glanced into the corner stall and noticed something partially hidden behind the rain barrel in the corner.

"Just a minute, Rawl, let me see what was left here in this far corner."

"Sure, Dawn, I'm on my way," replied Rawl coming up behind her.

With a squeal of delight, Dawn ran to the object in the corner. "Look, Rawl, it's Mother's old trunk. I wonder how it got here?"

Leaning over and taking a closer look, Rawl realized that it was the small trunk that he had thrown from the upstairs window during the fire. "I believe that it is the one that I threw from the upstairs bedroom window as I hastened out of the house during the fire. Yes, it is! I remember telling Dawson to salvage what they could from the house, and then I reminded him that I had thrown this out by the side of the house in the shrubbery. Apparently this was left unnoticed when the rest of what was salvaged was removed. We can take it now, and I'll store it for you at the academy until you have time to look through it."

"Oh, would you, Rawl, that would almost be like finding a part of my Mother again because I remember that this trunk was very special to her?" answered Dawn with a pleased look on her face.

"Sure thing! I'll go get the buggy. It won't take but a moment to load it on the back."

While waiting for Rawl to return, Dawn wondered what she would find inside the trunk, but that would have to wait for another day.

Soon they were driving though the entrance gates at Edisto-back to the new life that she was experiencing here at the academy. What a pleasant memory she would always have of this special day!

"Seek ye first the kingdom of God and His righteousness; and all these things shall be added unto you." Was this experience one of those things? She wondered ...

Chapter 32

Life at Edisto Continues

Following the rendezvous in the Four Oaks garden, it became a common occurrence to see Dawn and Rawl attending events at the academy together. They were often seen at the sporting activities as well as the social happenings. Even Robin approved because Rawl had always been very special to her. At first some eye brows were raised when the president of the academy was seen courting a widowed faculty member, but even the diehards finally accepted them as a couple.

Some mornings when Dawn awoke, she would pinch herself to see if it were really happening because Rawl was becoming more special to her each day. She soon began to recognize this special feeling as a deep and abiding love that was growing between her and this extraordinary man in her life.

She began to listen for the tap, tap, tap of his college ring on the side of her classroom door at the end of her last class of the day. He was always eager to hear of the progress of her students and encouraged her to tell him about any interesting incident that had happened during the day. Quite often there was an unusual happening that just sharing it with him made them both laugh which usually lessened the fatigue of the day for both of them.

"Rawl, why is it that you can make anything fun? I find myself looking for, and, yes, even expecting things to happen each day in class just so that I can share them with you the next time that we are together."

"I do it just to see that twinkle in your eyes. It's really the highlight of my day! Things in the president's office can get pretty serious and sometimes just plain boring."

With that said he took her hand and started to the dining hall for the supper meal.

Dawn found that she looked forward to being with him at meal time. It was disappointing for her when some days he needed to be away from the academy on business. She always felt that the day was incomplete when they couldn't be together at least for a little while.

There were just a few more weeks in the school year, and then Robin would be graduating and going away to college. It didn't seem possible that her daughter was almost a grown young woman and would be starting out on a life of her own very soon. Where had the time gone?

Robin had decided not to follow in her parents' footsteps and had been accepted at Furman, a school in the upper part of the state. They had an excellent Fine Arts department where she could pursue a degree in art and maybe take some music classes.

Wade's parents lived nearby, which would give her an opportunity to spend some time with her grandparents, much to their delight.

Chapter 33

A Turn of Events

Each time that Dawn and Rawl were together the subject of a lifetime commitment to each other would surface. They often parted with a prayer that God would lead them in this decision.

Falling in love with Rawl was easy because he was so considerate of her needs, always putting them above his own. He put no pressure on her to make a decision; however, his personality was so magnetic that she was drawn to him like a moth to a flame. She knew that it was not fair to compare the two men in her life because they were so different, but she couldn't help but be reminded of the deep struggle that she had had in making the decision to marry Wade because he was so persistent in pursuing her. The one thing that had attracted her to both of these men was their commitment to the Lord.

She had known since that day in the Four Oaks Garden that she and Rawl would someday be married. She did not want to detract in any way from Robin's special day of graduation, so she decided to wait until afterwards to make her decision known to everyone except Rawl. She tried to think of a unique way to tell him and so she asked him to meet her at the summer house at sunrise. Surely none of the students would be up at such an early hour, and they could be alone.

Being an early riser was no problem for her, but she wasn't sure about Rawl since their first encounter at the summer house years ago was at sunset.

Everything was quiet except the birds when she arrived first and sat in the gazebo to wait for Rawl. An early morning breeze was blowing through the open area. There was a rosy glow appearing over the horizon in the distance. She had only been there a few moments when she heard footsteps coming up behind her. She did hope that it was Rawl and not someone else. Turning away from the sunrise and toward the sound of the steps, she saw the smiling face that she was waiting to see.

"Good morning, Love of My Life! What was so important that you couldn't begin the day without telling me?" questioned a teasing Rawl.

"Come sit here beside me," she said as she patted the bench. "Do you see the sun beginning to rise over there behind those trees?" The sun was a fiery ball of orange as it rose to greet the day.

"I do. It's as pretty as a picture, and I should have brought my paint and brushes."

"Oh, no! You don't need that kind of paint. I want you to paint this sunrise in your memory because I want to tell you that this is the dawning of a new day in our lives. I really do love you, Rawl, and am finding you more irresistible each day. If you are still in agreement, I want to become Mrs. Rawl Manning."

He answered her by taking her in his arms and kissing her in such a way that she knew that he agreed.

After Rawl had been away on business for a few days, Dawn found a note on her desk one morning saying that he would be in to see her that afternoon following her last class of the afternoon. No reason was given! She found herself looking at the clock throughout the day. It had been hard to concentrate on the day's planned agenda because she was so looking forward to being with him again. It seemed like the day would never end. Finally the bell rang for the last class to be over. The students cleared out from her classroom. She was relieved that no one lingered for any further questions or discussion because she wanted to be free when Rawl came. With each passing footstep in the hallway, she looked up from her desk expecting to see his smiling face.

At last when she had become absorbed in grading some of the day's papers, she heard the familiar tap, tap, tap of Rawl's ring on her classroom door. Looking up she smiled and said, "Please come in. I have been waiting for you all day. You must have had lots of school business to keep you away for several days. I really have missed you."

"You are right. I have had a very busy schedule, but all of it has not been school concerns."

"Oh, and what else has been so important?" questioned a curious Dawn.

"This," said Rawl dropping down on one knee in front of her as he pulled a small box from his pocket and handed it to the surprised teacher before him. "We never really made our engagement official."

Dawn's hand was shaking a little as she slowly pressed the little pearl button on the side of the small blue velvet box that had just been placed in her hand. The lid popped open and there before her eyes was a beautiful diamond engagement ring. Rawl took it from her hand and placed it on her finger. "Now it is official; we are engaged to be married! I did get permission to do this by the way."

"Oh, really, have you been all the way to Charleston to see my father?" asked Dawn, a little surprised.

"Oh, no, I didn't have to go that far to get the answer I was looking for," answered Rawl teasing her.

"Then where DID you go for permission?"

"Right here on the campus! I asked someone whose opinion really mattered."

"And who might that be?"

"Your wonderful daughter, Robin! In fact she has been wanting to know when I was going to make this official. She even helped me know which ring to choose."

"You, two! Ganging up on me! I should have known."

At that moment who should appear at the door but the girl in question, Robin. "May I come in?" asked a sheepish inquirer.

"Please do," begged Rawl, "before I get in the dog house."

"Do you like it, Mama? Rawl made me feel so special when he asked me to help him decide."

"I really do! It makes it even more special knowing that he included you in the selection," answered her mother as she fought back a tear that began to roll down her cheek.

Looking down at her finger, she wondered what else she was going to discover about this extraordinary man that she was about to marry.

Now that Dawn and Rawl's engagement was official and the news was well known throughout the Edisto Campus, Dawn did her best to keep it low key for Robin's benefit. She had wanted to wait until after her daughter's graduation to share the news.

Then Robin could have received all the attention that was due her before the spotlight was turned on her mother again.

Chapter 34

Another Diploma is Earned

Just as it had been years ago when Dawn graduated, the Edisto campus was alive with activity on the morning of Robin's big day. Wade's parents had come and following the graduation exercises were taking Robin home with them for the summer. They were glad to know that Dawn had met someone that she could love and with whom she could spend the rest of her life. Of course, they had mixed emotions because they had loved their son, Wade, dearly. And this would close a chapter in their lives. Nevertheless the Stewarts concentrated on what was at hand, the graduation of their only granddaughter, Robin. The chapel in the academy was filled with proud parents, family, and friends.

Dawn sat with Wade's parents near the front in the reserved section.

Rawl, as the academy president, presided over the program on the platform. Following several speeches and the presentation of the awards, the diplomas were given to the waiting graduates.

Dawn was smiling radiantly when it was Robin's turn to walk across the stage. As Robin's given name was called, "Dawn Marie Stewart," she almost forgot that it was really her name and hesitated a moment. Rawl looked at her and then winked saying, "'Robin' Stewart as we all know her." She then quickly walked across the stage reaching out her hand to receive the diploma that was so well earned. Rawl grasped her hand firmly as he congratulated her. A special bond between them had grown over time.

In closing, the graduating seniors, for the last time, sang the school's alma mater with the student body.

The time had come for Robin to leave with her grandparents. Dawn promised Robin that she would write and share the wedding plans with her as they developed. She knew that it would be a small wedding in the school's chapel with only family and close friends present. They would have a brief honeymoon before returning to prepare for the fall term.

The Edisto campus was quiet and uneventful after the close of the school year.

Only a skeleton staff was left in charge of the academy during the summer months. This was a perfect time for Dawn to finalize her wedding plans. The first thing that she needed to do was write, Alice, her dear friend, who had encouraged this relationship from the beginning.

Finally, when she could be alone, Dawn sat down to pen the letter with the exciting news.

Dear Alice,

How are things with you? I do hope that you are doing well. Thank you for your wonderful support during our family's tragedies.

A lot of things have been happening here. Robin has graduated and is spending some time with Wade's parents before starting college in the fall. I have really enjoyed my work here at the academy. Rawl has been wonderful and so supportive.

You are not going to believe this, but Rawl and I plan to be married at the end of next month. Please plan to come. I have so much to tell you. It will be a small wedding with only family and a few close friends to help us celebrate the beginning of our life together. There are times when I have to pinch myself to see if I am dreaming.
    Looking forward to seeing you soon.
        Lovingly,
        Dawn

After dropping this letter in the mail, Dawn looked at her 'things to do' list for the next item of business. Checking them off one by one, she could see that there were only a few more items left undone.

A quiet early evening walk with Rawl became a top priority each day that it could be arranged. At supper Rawl reminded her that he would meet her at the summer house for their evening stroll. The campus was deserted for the summer which left them plenty of time to walk around the grounds without being disturbed. Even the birds were settling down for the night and had ceased their chirping.

Rawl could be seen coming across the campus toward the gazebo. There was a warm summer breeze blowing as he caught Dawn's hand when she stood to greet him.

They discussed many things concerning their future together. She felt such a sense of peace and completeness when she was in his presence. Often they would stop one more time at the summer house for a prayer before retiring for the evening, and thank God for the love that they had found in each other.

Walking back toward the main building, they noticed a full moon beginning to rise in the distance shining a bright light across their path. It began to be harder and harder for them to part at the close of the day. Rawl walked with her back to her room and after giving her one last embrace and good night kiss, they parted for the evening. Finally closing the door behind her, Dawn realized more and more that she too had found her soul-mate in Rawl.

Chapter 35

The Tapestry

Later in the summer, it became necessary for Rawl to be away from the academy to attend a conference concerning the fall school term. "This would be a good time to explore the contents of Mother's trunk," thought Dawn knowing that she would be alone most of the day. After sharing the idea with Rawl, he readily agreed.

Being a man of his word, she heard his familiar 'tap, tap, tap' on her room door early the following morning. Opening the door, she saw the small trunk sitting outside her room in the hallway. Rawl quickly announced, "I have an early morning delivery for My Lady," and with a wide sweep of his hand, he pointed to the trunk on the floor.

"Oh, Rawl, thank you so much! Please bring it in and place it over here by the window. It will be such fun to see what's inside with no one around to disturb me while I rummage through it. It will help to pass the time until you return," replied a very grateful Dawn.

Seeing the pleasure his thoughtful gesture brought her made leaving her for the day a little easier. After depositing the trunk where she requested, he quickly reached for her hand and pulled her to himself to give her a goodbye hug and kiss. Slowly, he released

The Rift of Dawn

her and started toward the door. Before leaving the room, he turned and with his charming smile and a wink insisted, "Now don't you get so lost in the past that you forget that I am in your future!"

Looking up, Dawn quickly responded, "Not a chance, I can hardly wait for my future to begin!"

As Rawl's footsteps disappeared down the hall, Dawn turned back to her mother's trunk and knelt beside it on the floor. The morning sunlight shone in from the open window and warmed her hand as she reached for the brass fastener on the side of the trunk. Her heart began to beat faster as she slowly raised the curved lid to reveal its contents.

There in the top tray lay what appeared at first glance to be her Edisto Academy diploma. Yes, it was, along with some other legal papers concerning the family property. To one side of the tray was a stack of letters that were yellow with age and tied together with a small blue ribbon. Looking closer she saw that the postmark was from the state of Virginia, and most of them were dated around 1863 and 1864. They were addressed to her maternal grandmother. Apparently these were letters received from her grandfather while he was fighting in Virginia. She recalled the story of his sending the apple seeds back in a letter and wondered which one held those memories. Reading the letters would have to wait until she could explore the remaining contents of the trunk.

Lifting out the tray and setting it gently aside, Dawn immediately saw the creamy yellow folds of her dress that Robin had worn in the portrait. How pleased she was to find that this treasure had escaped the ravenous fire that had destroyed so much of her past!

Because the trunk was so small, there was not much room to store anything else beside the yards of material that made up the billowy skirt. This was a disappointment to her, but on second glance there appeared to be a few more pieces folded in the bottom of the trunk.

Taking them out for a closer look, Dawn surmised that they were pieces of hand embroidery probably done by her grandmother. The stitches were delicately done with very little fading of the brilliant colors, probably because they were folded away from the sunlight for so many years.

Realizing that she had almost reached the bottom of her mother's keepsakes, she reluctantly laid the hand stitched pieces to one side.

Looking back, Dawn noticed one more piece in the far corner of the trunk. It appeared to be older than the others because it was so frayed. Pulling it out into the light to study it more carefully, she noticed dark and light green threads running helter-skelter across the material. Then there were large and small scarlet patches knotted with loose strains in various places here and there not making much sense of a pattern or design. There were also many small sharp brown stitches connected to long curved lines.

As she pondered the meaning of this strange piece, she began to wonder why it had been so important to her mother to keep it with the other obvious family keepsakes.

Before tossing it aside, she nonchalantly flipped it to the other side. Much to her surprise, the most beautiful cluster of several crimson roses and buds that she had ever seen appeared. They were among numerous pointed leaves attached to sturdy long stems with thorns on each side.

She gazed for a few moments at the beauty and wonder of the other side of the tapestry. Reflecting upon the parallel of what she had just witnessed and the events in her own life that at the time when they occurred made just as little sense, she began to realize that her perception and understanding of what God was weaving into her life fell far short of His wise plan, just as the underneath side of the tapestry had done.

It was then that the familiar verse, "All things work together for good to those who love God, to them who are the called according to His purpose," came to her mind. It was clear to her then that various kinds of experiences in our lives that are woven together form the complete pattern and plan that God designs. One day at His appointed time we will see the completed picture in its entirety!

As she once more viewed the upper side of the tapestry, it was almost as if she heard God say to her, "Behold! How I loved you!"

She knew then that this handiwork, whoever had originally designed it, would have to be framed and displayed in a prominent place in hers and Rawl's future home. And then each time that she saw it, she would be reminded that the plan that God has for our lives is wisest and best.

She could hardly wait for Rawl to come home so she could share this experience with him.

Later that afternoon, the shadows of the sun began to lengthen across the room as Dawn placed the aged letters back into the top tray of her mother's trunk. Reading them had given her a new insight into the lives of the ones who had lived before her. She wished that she could have known her grandparents; however, these letters allowed her to get a glimpse of their former lives.

Reluctantly, she closed the lid of the old trunk and glanced at the time. Surely Rawl would be back soon. It had been a long but interesting day. She decided to take a stroll around the campus and wait for him to return.

After a brisk walk, Dawn settled at her favorite spot on the grounds, the summer house, to look for Rawl. The afternoon sun began to sink lower behind the trees giving some relief from the summer heat that had been building throughout the day.

"Hello, Mrs. Stewart," called one of the maintenance men. "Waiting for Mr. Rawl? He should be back any time now. I usually meet him and take care of his horse and buggy."

"Why, yes, I am," answered Dawn, a little startled that she was not waiting alone. "He is expected back before dark."

As she spoke, horse's hooves could be heard approaching.

"There he is now. I'll take his horse to the stable so you can properly greet him," grinned the hired hand.

"Whoa!" called out Rawl as the horse came to a halt in front of the gazebo. Jumping down quickly from the buggy and giving the reins to the waiting hands, Rawl promptly came over to where Dawn was sitting.

"You look as if you have volumes to tell. There must have been some exciting things in that trunk!" exclaimed Rawl who was eager to hear a report.

"Oh, yes, it has been a wonderful day, and I can't wait to tell you about it," replied Dawn as she jumped up to greet him.

After a warm embrace, Rawl announced, "First let me take my things by the office and then I want to hear all about it."

Soon Dawn had related to her trusted confidante all the treasured keepsakes she had found in her mother's trunk.

Rawl was especially enthralled with her experience with the tapestry. He had studied her face intently as she shared with him the connection between scripture and the events in her life forming a completed design- God's design.

Finally, when there was a pause in her narrative of the happenings of the day, Rawl took her in his arms and whispered to her, "This is why I love you so, Dawn. There is a depth to you that only a few fortunate ones can fathom. And this depth can only come from knowing intimately the One who created you."

As twilight slowly fell around them, they, each one engrossed in his own thoughts, were grateful to be a part of God's masterpiece.

Chapter 36

A Letter from Robin

Following breakfast each morning, Dawn enjoyed a walk around the campus when she could experience that luxury. She often stopped for a brief rest at the summer house before beginning the activities of the day. Usually the timing was right to meet Rawl, who had gone nearby for the academy's mail.

Seeing Rawl coming up the drive, she called out, "Hello, Rawl, I'm over here. Any mail for me today?"

Hearing her voice, he looked up and said, "Just a moment, and I'll look. I think there was one here for you from Robin. Yes, here it is." With the letter in his hand, he walked over where she was waiting.

Just hearing her daughter's name brought Dawn quickly to her feet. She reached out, took the letter, and tore into the sealed envelope immediately.

Seeing that she was so quickly occupied with Robin's letter, Rawl, teasing her a bit, replied, "I can see that I am no longer needed here, so I shall continue on my journey with the mail."

Looking up, Dawn attempted an apology, "I'm so sorry, Rawl. I just am eager to see when she is coming. Our big day IS this coming Friday, you know! If you can wait a minute, I'll read it to you. I'm sure that there is a message here for you, also. There usually is. She is so fond of you."

Reaching for his hand, she pulled him over to one of the benches in the gazebo.

When they were both settled she read aloud:

Dear Mama,

I am writing to tell you that I shall be arriving on the 2 p.m. train on Wednesday. Please ask Rawl if he can come for me. Grandma and Grandpa will wait and come the morning of the wedding. This will give us a few days to catch up on the news and wedding plans before they arrive.

They have really been spoiling me. I think that I have seen all of Pa Pa's relatives. They took me shopping recently, and now I have everything that I need for college in the fall.

Grandma and I have been busy sewing my dress for the wedding. I really do like it, and I hope that you will, too. Grandpa says that I look beautiful!

I have missed you and Rawl very much. Tell Rawl to please not be a minute late because I can't wait to see you both.

Your loving daughter,
Robin

Looking up at Rawl, Dawn said, "Well, at least we know when she is coming, and usually the train is on time. Will this be a problem for you, Rawl, or do I need to make other arrangements to bring her home?"

"I wouldn't miss it for the world! In fact, we may need to have a private conversation, so if you have other things to do that day..." teased Rawl.

"Now, just hold on there, wild horses couldn't keep me away! This has been such a long summer without seeing her," commanded Dawn.

Smiling his intriguing smile, Rawl quickly retorted, "I didn't think that I had a chance, but you can't blame a guy for trying."

Standing up to leave, Rawl said, "This has been fun, but duty calls. I'll see you at lunch."

After a quick wave of her hand, Dawn picked up the letter again to enjoy it once more.

On the following Wednesday, Dawn and Rawl arrived early at the train station eager to see Robin. The train pulled into the station right on time. Robin waved wildly from the window as the train slowed to a stop.

Soon she was giving them both big hugs and chattering away about all that she had been doing.

As they drove into the academy entrance, Robin couldn't help but tease Rawl one more time. "Mama, Rawl hasn't tried to back out yet, has he? I was almost afraid to be gone so long for fear that he might." Glancing over at Rawl, she exclaimed, "Mama and I know a good catch when we see one, and I'm afraid that you have been caught!"

Entering into the lightheartedness of the moment, Rawl quickly replied, "So this is why your mother insisted on coming with me to get you. The two of you are ganging up on me this time to make sure that I don't get away. Well, at least you are warning me about what my life is going to be like with the two of you!"

"Yes," chimed in Dawn, "it's going to be quite an experience!"

Chapter 37

The Big Day Arrives

Finally her wedding day arrived. The air was somewhat humid as was typical this time of year, but there wasn't a cloud in the sky. Dawn had chosen to wear a light blue chiffon dress. Her hair was French braided with the lower part in a netted chignon. Small pink sweetheart roses were entwined in the braid and the netted chignon. She chose for her bouquet long stemmed pink rose buds. Her cherished daughter, Robin, was picture perfect in a matching pink dress. She was to be her only attendant.

The Edisto chapel was simply decorated with gladioli and ferns. Candles had been lighted for the late afternoon wedding. The guests were seated and eagerly anticipating the beginning of the ceremony.

Dawn waited with her father to enter the chapel. She still could not believe the turn of events in her life. There had been so much sadness in her life in recent years, that just the thought of spending the remainder of her life with Rawl brought tears of joy to her eyes.

The wedding music started; Robin was already in place at the altar. Dawn knew it was her turn. All eyes were on her as she walked down the aisle on her father's arm to meet Rawl whose eyes saw no one but her coming toward him.

The Rift of Dawn

The ceremony was brief and simple. The minister emphasized the sacredness of marriage that is ordained by God, and the two were joined together as one not to be separated.

Dawn, as she looked into Rawl's eyes, silently thanked God for giving her another wonderful husband to share her life.

It was then that she heard the preacher announce that they were husband and wife. Mr. And Mrs. Rawl Manning! Her heart was overwhelmed with unspeakable joy!

Following the ceremony, the wedding party and guests were invited into the dining hall for a sit down dinner prepared by the cafeteria staff.

Dawn and Rawl greeted each guest at the door receiving 'Congratulations!' from each one. Dawn looked radiant standing beside her new husband, and anyone could see how happy she was. Rawl, too, was no exception as he stood proudly beside that special someone that he had loved and admired for many years.

At last it was time to retire for the evening. Arrangements had been made for the guests who had traveled some distance to stay in the dormitory. After thanking each one for coming and saying, "Good night," Dawn and Rawl left to spend their first night together in the president's quarters which was Rawl's home and now would be Dawn's, also.

Chapter 38

The Dawning of a New Day

The next morning the newlyweds were up early as gracious hosts to see their guests off. Afterwards Dawn and Rawl left for a honeymoon trip to Savannah. Rawl had arranged for them to spend time at a relative's cottage on Tybee Beach.

The first morning there, being true to her name, Dawn wanted to witness a sunrise over the ocean. Grabbing a light jacket, she joined Rawl on the beach for an early morning stroll. There was a slight chill in the air as the breeze blew in from the sea. Rawl's strong arm felt good around her waist as they walked along the beach.

For a while they strolled along quietly, each one just enjoying being in the presence of the other.

Finally Dawn spoke as she pointed straight ahead, "Look, Rawl, the sun is just beginning to rise. Isn't it beautiful?"

And indeed it was! The sky was rosy pink with a bright glow of yellow rays ascending outward as the fiery red ball slowly began once again to appear above the horizon.

"God's mercies are new every morning and that is proof of it right there," commented Rawl, stopping to kiss his new bride there in the warmth of the early morning sun.

Work to prevent beach erosion was being done along the shore. There were bits and pieces of leftover Palmetto log pilings scattered along the beach. Rawl nonchalantly began kicking a small one along the sand. He laughed each time Dawn raced to roll it before he could. Before long they were back at the cottage. By this time Dawn had become quite attached to the foot long log and begged Rawl to keep it as a souvenir of this fun morning on the beach.

These few days of their honeymoon passed and became wonderful and precious memories for Dawn. Rawl had done everything that he could to let her know that even though there had been much that she had lost in her life, with him by her side, and God guiding them, there was still much to be gained in their future together. And so Dawn, at last began to realize, that even though the darkness of the night of her life's journey had been devastating, the dawn was giving way to morning splendor.

The Epilogue

Following Dawn and Rawl's trip to Savannah, they returned to the academy and served faithfully until the school was closed in 1934. The closing was done mainly because of the devastating effects of the Great Depression upon the economy and also the rise in popularity of public high schools.

It was under their influence that many of the students were led of God to enter into full time Christian vocations. Numerous students found their way to either foreign or home mission fields of service. Many future pastors and teachers received their inspiration for their life's calling at the academy. Little by little Dawn realized that even though the loss of Wade had been painful to her she at last saw the bigger picture of God's plan for her life. Because of her varied experiences, many others had been led to follow in the path of God's leading. For that she was grateful!

Robin received her degree in art and married her college sweetheart. In time they presented her mother with some much loved grandchildren.

For a while the descendants of the Randall family returned to the family cemetery to clean it and have annual reunions. It became a time of reminiscing and enjoying each other's fellowship. But as time marched on, fewer and fewer of them knew much about the Four Oaks Plantation of days gone by, and the cemetery, as well as the surrounding area, began to return to nature.

The casual observer today would notice little evidence that life had ever existed anywhere around except for the weathering tombstones in the fenced cemetery. Four giant live oak trees, still stand stately, but gnarled, almost a century later near where the house once stood seem proudly to uphold the Four Oaks Plantation name and heritage. Only one of the slave cabins remains in the distance.

To one side where once had been an immaculately manicured garden, the area is now overgrown with pines, scrub oaks, small brush, and weeds. But there at the entrance to the garden standing straight and tall, like a sentinel guarding the life it once witnessed, is a towering century plant, and yes, it is in full bloom.

Printed in the United States
47928LVS00003B/19-120

5/1/07 BQC